Frog

Mary Calmes
Art by Pyeongcho

DREAMSPINNER PRESS

Published by
DREAMSPINNER PRESS

5032 Capital Circle SW, Suite 2, PMB# 279, Tallahassee, FL 32305-7886 USA
www.dreamspinnerpress.com

This is a work of fiction. Names, characters, places, and incidents either are the product of author imagination or are used fictitiously, and any resemblance to actual persons, living or dead, business establishments, events, or locales is entirely coincidental.

Digital ISBN: 978-1-64108-019-4
Print ISBN: 978-1-64108-020-0
Published November 2018
v. 1.0

Printed in the United States of America
∞
This paper meets the requirements of
ANSI/NISO Z39.48-1992 (Permanence of Paper).

Chapter 1

THIS IS WEBER.

WEBER WHO?

WEBER?!

HMM...

CYRUS, DO YOU KNOW ANYBODY NAMED WEBER?

YOU KNOW WHAT, I'M SORRY...

SQUEEZING VERY HARD.

WEBER?

AH...

HEY, CYRUS.

SORRY FOR INTERRUPTIN' WITH WHATEVER YOU'RE DOIN'.

I WASN'T THINKIN'.

YOU'RE NOT INTERRUPTING ANYTHING. WHERE---

ARE YOU AT A PARTY?

NO, I'M JUST AT A FRIEND'S HOUSE, AND WE WERE ABOUT TO HAVE DINNER.

THEN, I'LL LET YOU EAT.

IT'S JUST A BIG GROUP, WEB. IT'S NOTHING.

WHAT A BEAUTIFUL VOICE...

I SEE.

WHERE ARE YOU?

NOT FAR, SO I THOUGHT I WOULD...

YES. COME SEE ME. I'LL GO HOME RIGHT NOW.

NO, THAT'S ALL RIGHT. I'LL JUST...

WEBER.

SIGH PLEASE. MEET ME THERE.

I'LL MEET YOU THERE IN THE MORNING.

WEBER, I'M SORRY, OKAY?

WHAT ARE YOU SORRY ABOUT? THERE'S NOTHING TO BE SORRY FOR.

BUT I UNDERSTOOD WHAT HE WAS SORRY FOR.

I'M NOT PUNISHING YOU. I JUST LOOK LIKE HELL.

I'D LIKE TO LOOK BETTER THIS TIME.

I PROMISE I'LL BE THERE TOMORROW.

YOU PROMISE?

YEAH.

I ALWAYS MET WITH CYRUS LOOKING LIKE HAMMERED SHIT.

HE DESERVED BETTER.

WEBER, YOU SOUND LIKE YOU'RE FREEZING. WHERE EXACTLY ARE YOU?

AT THE GREYHOUND BUS STATION IN OAKLAND.

I DON'T WANNA INTERRUPT YOUR---

I'LL BEG. DO YOU WANT ME TO BEG?

* POURING RAIN *

YOU'RE THAT CLOSE?

I DON'T GIVE A DAMN WHAT YOU LOOK LIKE. JUST LET ME COME GET YOU, PLEASE?

NO, NOT EVER.

I'M SO SORRY ABOUT LAST TIME...

ABOUT SEVEN MONTHS AGO, WHEN I WAS READY TO GO TO RENO, CYRUS GAVE ME AN ULTIMATUM.

STAY FOREVER OR GO AND NEVER COME BACK. I HAD TO CHOOSE.

I WAS SURPRISED THAT A MAN LIKE CYRUS WOULD EVEN WANT A GUY LIKE ME.

I HAD ACTUALLY FORGOTTEN THE FIGHT...

OH, SHIT, CYRUS. I SHOULDN'T HAVE BOTHERED YOU.

WEBER.

I'M SO STUPID. TALK ABOUT A NEEDY BASTARD.

GOD, I'M SUCH AN ASS.

NO!

WEBER YATES! DON'T YOU DARE HANG UP!

...

YEAH, BUT---

I WANT TO SEE YOU!

...

CYRUS, STOP YOUR YELLIN'. YOUR FRIENDS ARE GONNA THINK YOU'RE GOING CRAZY.

I DON'T CARE! WEB, JUST---

ARE YOU SURE YOU WANNA SEE ME? YOU AIN'T MAD NO MORE?

YES, SO SURE... I WANT TO SEE YOU SO MUCH. I WAS NEVER MAD.

* COUGHS SOFTLY *

I SHOULDN'T HAVE CALLED...

THE GUY WHO ANSWERED THE PHONE, WAS THAT THE GUY?

WHAT GUY?

LAST TIME WE TALKED, YOU SAID YOU WERE FIXIN' TO GET SERIOUS WITH A GUY WHO WANTED A COMMITMENT CEREMONY WITH YOU...

NO... THAT WASN'T HIM. IT'S BEEN OVER FOR SIX MONTHS. TURNS OUT, YOU CAN'T LOVE SOMEONE JUST BECAUSE YOU SHOULD.

'CAUSE I DON'T WANNA MESS NOTHIN' UP FOR YA. I RECKON I PUT YOU THROUGH ENOUGH.

WEBER, THERE'S NOTHING TO MESS UP. I'M SO SORRY FOR HOW WE PARTED WAYS.

BABY, I'M SO SORRY FOR WHAT I SAID.

YOU KNOW, I'M KINDA TORN UP.

MAYBE THIS WASN'T SUCH A GOOD---

IT WAS! IT WAS A GREAT IDEA!

REALLY NICE OF YOU TO NOT LET ME FEEL LIKE AN ASSHOLE FOR THE REST OF MY LIFE.

YOU'RE NOT AN ASSHOLE.

LAST TIME, I WENT AFTER YOU, BUT YOU WERE ALREADY GONE.

YOU DID? IT'S NICE TO HEAR.

YES. I REALLY AM SO SORRY.

FORGET IT. I'LL SEE YOU.

WHEN?

HE KNEW ME WELL FOR SOMEONE WHO HAD SEEN ME MAYBE FIFTEEN TIMES IN A THREE-YEAR PERIOD.

I DON'T KNOW... IF IT'S NOT TOO MUCH TROUBLE, COULD YOU COME FETCH ME AT THE STATION?

OKAY. I'LL BE RIGHT THERE. DON'T LEAVE. PLEASE.

HE KNEW TO ASK ME FOR A DEFINITIVE TIMELINE. OTHERWISE MY WORDS COULD HAVE MEANT TODAY, TOMORROW, OR BEFORE I DIED.

IT AIN'T LIKE YOU TO WORRY.

NO, I KNOW. I JUST... I MISSED YOU, AND I DIDN'T HAVE ANY WAY TO REACH... I'M JUST SO GLAD YOU CALLED. YOU HAVE NO IDEA.

CYRUS AND I MET IN TEXAS.

I WAS BREAKING HORSES ON A RANCH BETWEEN RODEOS.

CYRUS AND SOME OF HIS FRIENDS WERE CLIENTS WHO CAME TO HUNT QUAIL.

* SCRAPING SOUND *
끼이―

THE GUIDE RESPONSIBLE FOR THEM WAS HELD UP, SO MY BOSS AT THE TIME ASKED ME TO RUN INTO TOWN AND PICK THEM UP.

HE WAS WEARING A SUIT THAT COST MORE THAN ALL MY EARTHLY POSSESSIONS PUT TOGETHER.

* GLANCE *

* VROOM *

* SIGH OF RELIEF *

WHAT WAS YOUR NAME?

...

WEB. WEBER YATES. WHAT'S YOURS?

CYRUS.

THIS MAN WAS BY FAR...

CYRUS BENNING.

...THE MOST BEAUTIFUL THING I HAD EVER SEEN IN MY LIFE.

HMM...

I DON'T NORMALLY DO THIS KIND OF THING...

AND YOU'RE PROBABLY NOT...

BUT DO YOU THINK YOU MIGHT WANT TO HAVE DINNER WITH ME?

SINCE I WANTED TO JUMP HIM,

I KNEW I WOULDN'T MA IT THROUGH DINNER.

OR WE COULD JUST FIND A MOTEL AND FUCK?

...

THAT'S NOT REAL SAFE IN THIS TOWN. RUMORS SPREAD FAST.

WE COULD DO THAT.

BUT I'D ALSO LOVE TO FEED YOU IF YOU'D LET ME.

* MOVEMENT *

OKAY THEN, ROOM SERVICE AND SEX, IT IS.

WHEN ARE YOU FREE?

I GET OFF WORK AT SIX.

SO, SEVEN THEN?

* NOD *

Chapter 2

NO ONE COMES HERE AT THIS TIME OF THE DAY.

GET THOSE PANTS DOWN AND THAT SHIRT OFF.

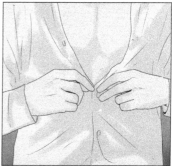

* SOUND OF CLOTHES RUSTLING *

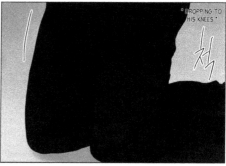

* DROPPING TO HIS KNEES *

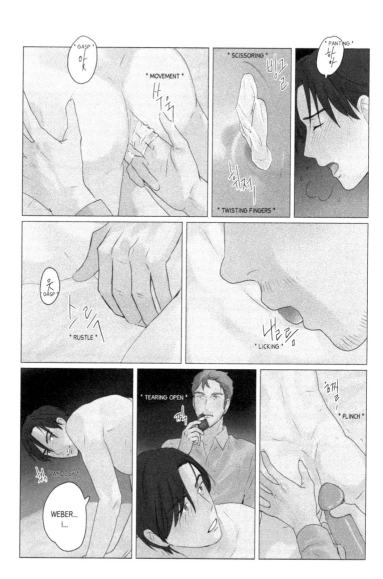

Chapter 3

SINCE WHEN DO YOU CRY FOR ME?

SINCE I NEVER THOUGHT I'D SEE YOU AGAIN.

MISSED YOU. ALWAYS.

Chapter 4

Chapter 5

YAY!
YAY!
* ELECTRONIC SOUNDS *
* ELECTRONIC SOUNDS *

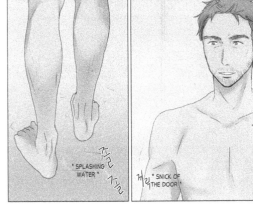

* SPLASHING WATER *

YOU CAN'T COME IN. YOU HAVE TO MAKE DINNER FOR THEM BOYS.

* SNICK OF THE DOOR *

Chapter 6

WHAT?

OH, I SEE.

NO, THAT'S OKAY.

I WAS SO STUPID.

I CALLED THE GUY IN ALASKA TO TELL HIM I COULDN'T COME DUE TO PERSONAL REASONS, AND HE WAS SURPRISED TO HEAR FROM ME. APPARENTLY MY FRIEND HADN'T TALKED TO HIM ABOUT ME.

SO I'D CROSSED THE COUNTRY ON A MAYBE INSTEAD OF A FOR SURE AND COULD HAVE KICKED MYSELF. I KNEW BETTER.

MY "FRIEND" HAD JUST WANTED TO GET IN MY PANTS AND USED THE JOB OFFER TO DO IT. I REALLY WASN'T VERY BRIGHT.

MY FRIEND'S BROTHER WAS EMBARRASSED, BUT HE HAD MADE NO PLANS TO HIRE SOMEONE. HE THOUGHT THERE MIGHT BE A JOB IN ANOTHER COUPLE OF WEEKS OR SO, BUT HE COULDN'T SAY FOR CERTAIN.

* DISBELIEVING LAUGH *

* PEEKS *

I AM SO STUPID, LITTLE MAN.

NO, YOU'RE NOT! LIZZIE IN MY CLASS, SHE'S STUPID. SHE EATS HER BOOGERS.

YOU DON'T DO THAT. I'VE BEEN WATCHING.

GRUNTING

* SQUEAL *

YOU WANNA GET THE REMOTE?

NOPE. YOU WANNA GET IT?

NOPE.

CALL MICAH!

MICAH!

* HURRIED STEPS *

* MOVEMENT *

THANK YOU.

* HUDDLING TOGETHER *

* ELECTRONIC SOUNDS *

WHAT'RE YOUR MOM AND UNCLE CY DOIN'?

DRINKING TEA AND TALKING.

ELECTRONIC SOUNDS (GAME CONSOLE)

I SEE. TALKING IS SO BORING.

SO TRUE.

HAHA.

UH?

THE BOYS?

CAROLYN TOOK THEM HOME. THEY DIDN'T WANT TO LEAVE. IT WAS A STRUGGLE.

HOW LONG WAS I ASLEEP?

COUPLE OF HOURS.

YOU SHOULD GET UNDER THE COVERS AND GO TO SLEEP. YOU'RE EXHAUSTED.

I DIDN'T. SHE DECIDED ALL ON HER OWN THAT YOU WERE TO BE TRUSTED.

THANK YOU FOR ASKING YOUR SISTER TO TAKE PITY ON ME.

IT MAKES NO SENSE.

YOU KNOW WHAT REALLY DOESN'T MAKE SENSE? THAT YOU WON'T JUST STAY WITH ME AND LET ME TAKE CARE OF YOU.

I CAN'T DO THAT.

SIGH

CYRUS.

LET GO.

* GRABBING *

IF I HAD ANYTHING TO OFFER AT ALL, I'D LAY CLAIM TO HIM.

BUT I WAS A HOMELESS DRIFTER AND I WOULD ONLY BE A DIVERSION UNTIL CYRUS MET A BETTER PERSON.

WEBER, STOP.

REALITY WASN'T A FAIRYTALE.

* SIGH OF PLEASURE *

ㅎ아

* KISSING SOUND *

쪽쪽

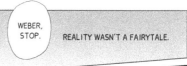

CYRUS, TAKE OFF YOUR CLOTHES.

NO.

GET UNDER THE DAMN COVERS SO I CAN HOLD YOU WHILE YOU SLEEP.

HE WAS...REALLY WORRIED ABOUT ME.

꾸욱

* SQUEEZING *

COME HERE.

* FLOPS BACK *

털썩

* GASP *

YOU'RE THE ONLY ONE WHO KNOWS I LOVE IT, BECAUSE YOU'RE THE ONLY ONE WHO EVER MADE ME DO IT.

THE FIRST TIME I'D CUDDLED WITH HIM, HE HAD TRIED TO SQUIRM AWAY.

NO ONE BUT YOU EVER HOLDS ME LIKE THIS.

DUMB FUCKERS. THEY'RE MISSIN' OUT ON SOMETHIN' GREAT.

BUT AS I HELD HIM PRESSED TO MY HEART, I HAD FELT HIM SURRENDER. HE WAS A NATURAL SNUGGLER.

YOU'RE THE ONLY ONE WHO HAD THE BALLS TO TRY TO MAKE ME SUBMIT.

THAT'S RIGHT.

THANK YOU FOR WANTING TO HOLD ME, WEBER.

THANK YOU FOR LETTIN' ME, CYRUS.

DID YOU SLEEP WELL?

MA'AM.

YOUR CHILDREN ARE EVIL.

* LAUGHING *

DID YOU WAKE UP WITH THEIR FREEZING LITTLE FEET ON YOUR STOMACH?

I DID.

* LAUGHING *

HAHA. IT MEANS THEY REALLY DO LIKE YOU.

HOW DID YOU SLEEP, COWBOY?

I PROMISED MY FOLKS I WOULD SPEND THE WEEKEND WITH THEM.

MY BROTHER BRETT AND HIS FAMILY ARE SPENDING THE HOLIDAYS WITH HIS WIFE'S FAMILY. WE WON'T SEE THEM AGAIN UNTIL AFTER THE NEW YEAR.

OKAY.

AIN'T A COWBOY NO MORE.

YOU'LL ALWAYS BE MY COWBOY.

CAROLYN AND THE KIDS ARE SUPPOSED TO GO AS WELL.

I WAS SUPPOSED TO GO THERE WITH MY HUSBAND.

THAT AIN'T YOUR FAULT, CAROLYN.

* DEEP SIGH *

I KNOW, BUT STILL...

TAKE THE KIDS AND GO THERE, CAROLYN. I CAN STAY HERE.

* KISS SOUND *

COME WITH US, WEBER. I WANT YOU TO SPEND MORE TIME WITH THE BOYS.

AND I WANT TO TALK TO YOU ABOUT MICAH.

I DON'T WANNA BE IN THE WAY.

YOU WON'T BE. BELIEVE ME, BOTH MY BROTHER AND I NEED YOU AS A BUFFER FROM OUR PARENTS.

IS THAT RIGHT?

MY FATHER AND I ARE DIFFERENT KINDS OF MEN, AND MY MOTHER WORRIES ABOUT ME INCESSANTLY.

SO YOU GET THAT FROM HER, DO YOU?

MEANING WHAT?

WHY DOESN'T MICAH TALK?

CAN'T YOU RECOGNIZE IT?

THAT DOESN'T COUNT. ANYONE IN THEIR RIGHT MIND WOULD WORRY ABOUT YOU.

AH...

A LITTLE OVER A YEAR AGO, HE WAS AT HOME WITH MY MOTHER-IN-LAW BECAUSE HE DIDN'T WANT TO GO TO TRISTAN'S SOCCER GAME WITH THE REST OF US. SHE HAD A HEART ATTACK AND DIED.

SHE HAD AN ACUTE PULMONARY EMBOLISM. SHE WAS GONE IN A MATTER OF SECONDS. MICAH CALLED 911, AND THAT WAS THE LAST TIME HE'S SPOKEN.

HE WAS WITH HER ALONE UNTIL THE AMBULANCE CAME?

YES.

AND HOW LONG WAS THAT?

NOT LONG. TEN MINUTES, MAYBE.

THAT'S LONG FOR A LITTLE KID.

YOU'RE RIGHT. HE HASN'T UTTERED A WORD IN ALMOST A YEAR.

YES!

YOU HAV TO EAT T ITEM.

I SUSPECT HE'LL COME CRYIN' BACK TO YOU ONCE HE FIGURES OUT THAT THE NANNY AIN'T A WOMAN BUT A GIRL INSTEAD.

WHEN HE COMES BACK, YOU GOT YOURSELF A DECISION TO MAKE.

* SOB *

* SOB *

I HAVEN'T BEEN HELD LIKE THIS IN FOREVER.

I AM SO SORRY TO HEAR THAT. BEIN' HELD IS ONE OF THE BEST PARTS OF HAVIN' A MATE.

* SNIFFLES *

* SQUEEZING HARD *

* DEEP SIGH *

YOU'RE RIGHT. THAT'S TRUE.

I GET WHY CYRUS LOVES YOU.

* JOLT *

SO NOW I UNDERSTAND.

MICAH DIDN'T SAVE HIS GRANDMOTHER, SO HE FEELS LIKE HE FAILED.

EXACTLY.

THAT'S
WHAT HIS
THERAPIST
THINKS.

* NOD *
끄덕

HE FEELS
LIKE HE
SHOULD HAVE
DONE
SOMETHIN'.

MICAH,
JUST
THERE!

* LAUGHING *
까까

MICAH...

YOU'VE
BEEN
HURTING...

쿡쿡
* LAUGHING *

헤헤
* HEHE *

Chapter 7

IS IT ENOUGH?

* LOADED BAGS *

YES.

HOW IS THIS COAT?

IT'S GREAT. THAT COAT IS HOT.

I KNOW, RIGHT? IT WOULD LOOK GOOD ON YOU, WEBER.

A COAT IS A COAT.

CAN I GET YOU DRESS SHOES?

NO.

YOU'LL NEED THEM.

FOR WHAT?

I HAVE A DINNER TO GO TO WHILE YOU'RE HERE.

JUST A PAIR OF BLACK LACE-UPS TO KEEP AT MY HOUSE?

NO.

I DON'T KNOW WHERE YOUR DINNER IS BUT I'LL STAY HOME.

I MEAN, I'LL STAY AT YOUR HOUSE.

* GASP *

YOU SAID "HOME".

YOU KNOW WHAT I MEANT.

IT WAS NICE, HOW IT SOUNDED.

CYRUS!

* ABRUPTLY *

STOP DOING THIS! YOU KNOW I WOULD STICK AROUND IF THERE WAS SHIT I COULD DO IN SAN FRANCISCO, BUT THERE AIN'T! I WON'T LIVE ON YOU AND BE A WHORE!

JESUS.

SHIT.

LETTING ME TAKE CARE OF YOU WOULD NOT MAKE YOU A WHORE, WEBER.

BUT IF I CAN'T PROVIDE FOR MYSELF, I CAN'T RESPECT MYSELF. AND HOW CAN YOU RESPECT ME IF I DON'T? YOU'D COME TO HATE ME.

NO, I WOULDN'T.

YOU WOULD. AND I WON'T TAKE THAT CHANCE.

WEBER...

I JUST WON'T.

OKAY. ANYWAY, I WANT YOU AT THAT PARTY WITH ME, SO I'LL GET THE SHOES.

YOU WEAR THEM, AND I'LL KEEP THEM. HOW'S THAT?

AGREED.

CYRUS, LET'S GO. YOUR PARENTS WILL BE WAITING FOR US.

FINE.

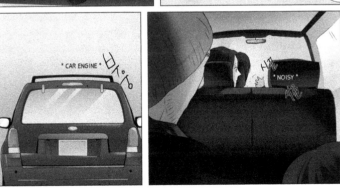

* CAR ENGINE *

* NOISY *

* NODDING *

WOW, YOU'RE SAYING THAT I LOOK LIKE A RHINOCEROS?

* LAUGHING *

* SHAKING *

* CLEARS HIS THROAT *

YEAH.

* CAR DOOR SHUTS *

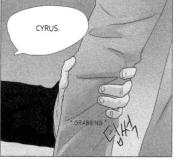

CYRUS.

* GRABBING *

I DON'T WANT US TO FIGHT NO MORE. LET'S STOP BEING MISERABLE ALONE AND KISS AND MAKE UP.

* LITTLE KISSES *

OH YES. YOU'RE GOING TO BE SO SORRY. WHEN YOU'LL WANT US TO BE ALONE, I'LL LEAVE YOU HANGING.

HOW SO?

YOU ARE SO GOING TO WANT MY ASS, AND I'LL BE DAMNED IF YOU'LL GET IT.

MAYBE IT'S ABOUT TIME YOU HAD MINE.

HEAVY FOOTSTEPS

FREEZE

YOURS?

YES, MINE.

YOUR ASS?

WHOOSH

WE'VE ESTABLISHED THIS.

YOU SAID YOU'VE NEVER TRUSTED ANYONE ELSE ENOUGH TO LET THEM TOP.

THAT'S RIGHT.

JESUS, WEBER!

SO YOU'RE SAYING YOU TRUST ME THAT MUCH?

THAT'S WHAT I'M SAYIN'. YESSIR.

WHEN HAVE YOU EVER KNOWN ME TO DO SUCH A THING?

NEVER.

YOU'RE NOT TEASING ME?

THEN IT MEANS...THAT I'LL BE YOUR FIRST?

THE FIRST AND ONLY, I SUSPECT. TRUST DOESN'T COME EASY TO ME.

WEBER, DO YOU HAVE ANY IDEA HOW BEAUTIFUL YOUR EYES ARE?

THEY'RE JUST FADED BLUE, LIKE JEANS. YOURS ARE SOMETHIN' TO SEE.

Chapter 8

CYRUS!

FATHER, MOTHER!

HOW ARE YOU?

IT'S BEEN A LONG TIME

BUZZING

WEBER!

JUMPING

THESE ARE MY COUSINS.

I'M VANESSA.

I'M VICTORIA.

THEY'RE UNCLE BRETT AND AUNTIE RACHEL'S DAUGHTERS.

THEY'RE REALLY CUTE.

I'M WEBER YATES, A FRIEND OF YOUR UNCLE CYRUS.

* GRIN *

멍!

* BARKING *

* WAGGING TAIL *

* PANTING *

* BREATHES OUT *

* BALL HITS THE GROUND *

* ROLLING *

THROW IT FAR AWAY!

* MOVEMENT *

IT'S AWFULLY NICE OF YOU TO BE OUT HERE WATCHING MY GRANDCHILDREN WHILE THE OTHERS ARE IN THERE TALKING.

HE LOOKS SO MUCH LIKE CYRUS.

* EXTENDS HIS HAND *

IT'S MY PLEASURE. THESE KIDS ARE ADORABLE.

NICE TO MEET YOU.

* PANTING *

* SQUEAL *

* WAGGING *

DID YOU COME WITH CYRUS?

YES, HIM AND CAROLYN, SIR.

HOW IS SHE?

I THINK SHE'S DEALING WITH IT AND BEING BRAVE FOR HER BOYS.

SWEETHEART!

DARLIN', DON'T PULL ON HIS EARS OR PUT YOUR FACE RIGHT UP TO HIS, ALL RIGHT?

* SURPRISED *

* SQUEEZING *

* PANTING *

* WHOOSH *

YES WEBER!

* PANTING *

EXCUSE ME, SIR.

GO AHEAD.

I'M NOT SCOLDIN' YOU, YOU UNDERSTAND?

NO, I KNOW.

* NOD *

YOU JUST DON'T WANT ME TO GET BITTEN.

* MOVEMENT *

THAT'S RIGHT.

* FOCUSED *

WEBER, TRISTAN SAID I CAN'T BE A FIREMAN. IS THAT TRUE?

NO, OF COURSE THAT'S NOT TRUE. YOU CAN BE WHATEVER YOU PLEASE.

I KNOW, RIGHT? THAT'S WHAT I TOLD HIM.

YOU DID WELL.

WEBER.

WILL YOU TELL GRANDPA TO LET ME RIDE THE HORSEY?

SHOULDN'T YOU ASK HIM YOURSELF?

ME?

I'LL GO WITH YOU. LET'S SEE WHAT HE SAYS.

GRANDPA.

YES?

YOU SURE
YOU DON'T
WANNA COME?

* NODDING *

ALL RIGHT,
THEN.

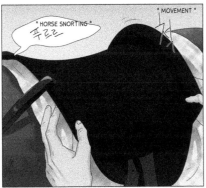

* HORSE SNORTING *

* MOVEMENT *

HELLO.

NICE TO MEET YOU, I'M RACHEL.

I'M WEBER, CYRUS'S FRIEND.

SHE'S VANESSA AND VICTORIA'S MOTHER.

MY KIDS ARE ALREADY FOLLOWING YOU EVERYWHERE.

THEY'RE LOVELY GIRLS.

YOU SEEM TO BE GREAT WITH THEM.

AUNTIE, WHO'S THAT MAN? THE ONE STANDING BY UNCLE CYRUS.

AH, THAT'S A FRIEND OF YOUR UNCLE BRETT'S. HE'S THE PERSON MEETING CYRUS THIS WEEKEND.

IF WE HAD KNOWN YOU WERE COMING WITH CYRUS, WE WOULDN'T HAVE INVITED HIS FRIEND.

OF COURSE, NO PROBLEM HERE.

* MOVEMENT *

HOLD ON TIGHT.

HEHE, THAT'S SO COOL. COME ON, MOUNT UP. LET'S RIDE FAST!

HIYA!

* LAUGHING *
까하아

* MOVEMENT *

OH...

* HOOFBEATS *

WE'RE GONNA RIDE SLOWLY BECAUSE I DON'T WANT YOU TO GET HURT.

WHAT A BEAUTIFUL HOME.

* HORSE WALKING *

THE STABLE IS NICER THAN SOME OF THE BEST HOTELS I SLEPT IN...AND PEOPLE ARE KIND.

CYRUS'S FATHER IS MAKING AN EFFORT TO TALK WITH ME, AND RACHEL... THEY'RE GREAT.

CYRUS IS THAT IMPORTANT.

YOU'RE RIDING REALLY WELL.

DO YOU WORK WITH HORSES?

I WAS WORKING AS A RANCH HAND.

NO WONDER YOU'RE A GREAT RIDER.

FEET TOUCHING THE GROUND

BE CAREFUL.

WAS IT FUN?

I WASN'T ASHAMED OF MY JOB.

YES!

NODDING

I DIDN'T USE TO HAVE REGRETS, BUT THESE DAYS I WAS FEELING ODD.

GREAT.

Chapter 9

MICAH! UNCLE WILL CATCH YOU.

WHAT'S HAPPENING?

HE'S SCARED AND WON'T GET DOWN.

WE'VE BEEN TRYING TO COAX HIM DOWN BUT HE JUST WON'T.

TREMBLING

MICAH!

COLD, AIN'T IT?

WELL, IF YOU'RE COMIN', HURRY UP AN' LET GO. YOU KNOW I'LL CATCH YA.

MICAH, YOU CAN
DO THAT, RIGHT?

* NODDING *

* WHOOSH *

* LANDING HARD *

* WIND KNOCKED
OUT OF HIM *

YOU'RE SAD YOU DIDN'T GO RIDIN' NOW, AREN'T YA?

* NODDING *

NEXT TIME TELL ME THE TRUTH IF YOU'RE STUCK. YOU GOT NO CALL TO BE LYIN' TO ME.

* HOLDING TIGHT *

ANYWAY, YOU'RE SAFELY BACK ON THE GROUND. LET'S GO BACK INSIDE.

* SQUEEZING VERY HARD *

HELLO, MA'AM.

OH, HELLO.

I'M CYRUS'S MOTHER. PLEASE, CALL ME ANGIE.

I'M WEBER, CYRUS'S FRIEND.

OH YES, CAROLYN SAID YOU WERE COMING.

IT'S A PLEASURE TO MEET YOU.

FOR ME AS WELL, MA'AM.

WOULD YOU LIKE SOME LEMONADE?

THAT WOULD BE GREAT, THANK YOU.

* SQUEEZING *

THAT WAS WONDERFUL OUTSIDE.

WHAT WAS?

* SOUND OF HER HAND PRESSING ON THE LEMON *

DROPS FALLING *

AND YOU HAVE NO IDEA WHAT YOU... OH BOY.

MY GRANDCHILDREN ARE ALL IN LOVE WITH YOU, AS WELL AS MY DOGS.

I DO WELL WITH KIDS AND ANIMALS. THEY DON'T CARE 'BOUT THE SAME THINGS ADULTS DO.

BUT...

...ADULTS' PERCEPTION ARE ALSO IMPORTANT.

* MOVEMENT *

YES, THEY ARE.

HERE'S YOUR DRINK.

THANK YOU.

PARDON ME, BUT WHERE IS THE RESTROOM?

DOWN THIS HALLWAY. IT WILL BE ON YOUR RIGHT.

THANK YOU.

* POURING WATER *

EARLIER, CYRUS AND HIS BROTHER'S FRIEND WERE LOOKING GOOD TOGETHER.

MY NOSE HAS BEEN BROKEN MANY TIMES. I HAVE A SQUARE JAW AND THIN LIPS.

WHY DOES CYRUS WANT ME?

COMING ALONG WITH HIM WAS A MISTAKE.

* FREEZES *

먼춧

ROSS, I'M SORRY.

IT'S FINE. WE'LL TRY AGAIN WHEN THE COWBOY LEAVES.

OF COURSE I WOULD. YOU HAVE NO IDEA HOW HOT YOUR BROTHER IS, AND ON TOP OF THAT, HE'S A NEUROSURGEON.

FORGET IT. YOU HAD NO IDEA YOUR BROTHER WAS INTO GUYS LIKE THAT.

저벅

REALLY? YOU'D GIVE THIS ANOTHER SHOT?

YOU'RE A STOCKBROKER. YOU MAKE A GOOD SALARY. WHAT DO YOU CARE?

SHIT.

* HEAVY FOOTSTEPS *

저벅

BECAUSE I'D LIKE TO DATE SOMEONE WHO HAS THEIR OWN MONEY AND ISN'T LOOKING FOR ME TO TAKE CARE OF THEM.

I'M REALLY GLAD TO BE ONE OF YOU AND RACHEL'S ONLY SINGLE GAY FRIENDS SO I COULD HAVE THE CHANCE TO MEET YOUR BROTHER.

BUT WASN'T CYRUS A COMPLETE DICK TO YOU?

I JUST THOUGHT THAT YOU TWO WOULD MAKE A GREAT COUPLE.

GIVE IT A REST. I'M GAY AND YOUR BROTHER'S GAY--- THAT'S ALL YOU THOUGHT.

THE MAN IS A WORLD CLASS SURGEON. I THINK THE ICE QUEEN THING IS PART OF IT. YOU DON'T SEE IT BECAUSE YOU'RE FAMILY, BUT I BET THAT'S HOW HE IS WITH EVERYONE HE DOESN'T KNOW WELL.

MAYBE.

I DIDN'T EVEN KNOW CYRUS KNEW SOMEONE LIKE WEBER WHOEVER.

SEE, YOU NEVER REALLY KNOW YOUR OWN FAMILY.

I GUESS NOT.

I'M SURPRISED MY FOLKS EVEN LET HIM BRING HIM IN THE HOUSE.

SO AM I.

. . . . . .

DINNER IS READY.

* CHATTERING *

* LAUGHING *

* HO-HO *

* CLINK *

* GETTING UP *

* RATTLE *

WHERE ARE YOU GOING?

I'M DONE EATING?

OH?

WHAT?

* FUMING *

* GLANCING *

* WHOOSH *

YOU'RE BEING DISRESPECTFUL BY ANSWERING LIKE THAT.

DON'T SAY 'WHAT'. SAY 'PARDON ME'.

YOU'RE NOT MY FATHER.

NO, SIR, I AM NOT.

GRANDMA.

YES, TRIS?

THE CHICKEN WAS REALLY GOOD.

THANK YOU FOR MAKING IT. MAY I PLEASE BE EXCUSED?

YES, YOU MAY.

* NOD *

ㄲㄷ

GRANDMA, ME AND MICAH LIKED THE FOOD TOO. CAN WE GO?

YES, DEAR.

* EXULTANT *

DID I DO GOOD?

* TOUSLING HIS HAIR *

YESSIR, YOU DID REALLY WELL.

* RUNNING WATER *

* STEADY MOVEMENT *

I'M SORRY.

NOTHIN' TO BE SORRY FOR.

ARE YOU MAD?

NO, SIR. WOULD YOU HELP ME WITH THE DISHES?

YESSIR.

YOU DID WELL TRIS, I'M PROUD OF YOU.

* SPEECHLESS *

I AM ENJOYING HAVING YOU HERE VERY MUCH, WEBER. WE HAVEN'T HAD MANNERS IN THIS HOUSE FOR SOME TIME.

OH YES, MA'AM, I AM AWARE.

IT'S ONE THING IF THE CHILDREN DON'T KNOW BETTER.

IT'S MORE OF AN ISSUE WHEN ADULTS DON'T HAVE MANNERS.

HUM-HUM!

* COUGHING *

I NEED TO SPEAK TO YOU RIGHT NOW.

BUT I'M WASHING THE---

LEAVE IT.

* SURPRISED *

BRETT AND RACHEL CAN TAKE OVER.

THANK YOU, MOTHER.

LET'S TALK...

Chapter 10

I HAD NO IDEA THAT MAN WAS GOING TO BE HERE.

WHAT MAN?

YOU'RE AN ASS.

* WHOOSH *

I DIDN'T, THOUGH. I WOULD NEVER TRY TO MAKE YOU JEALOUS.

YES, I KNOW THAT.

WHEN YOU'RE WITH ME, YOU'RE THE ONLY ONE I SEE.

WHICH IS REAL NICE TO HEAR.

* KISSING SOUND *

* WHINE *

* MOANING *

* PANTING *

* HOLDING TIGHT *

WERE YOU JEALOUS?

PARDON?

EVEN THOUGH I HAD NOTHING TO DO WITH IT, YOU'RE JEALOUS OF WHAT'S HIS NAME.

ROSS.

WE BELIEVE TWO COMPLETELY DIFFERENT TRUTHS.

I---

WHAT? TELL ME.

EVEN WHEN I'M GONE--- THAT GUY DOESN'T DESERVE YOU.

SAY WHAT YOU MEAN.

DON'T EVER KISS HIM OR FUCK HIM OR DO ANYTHING WITH HIM AT ALL.

I PROMISE.

IT'S NICE THAT YOU'RE MAKING DEMANDS.

SHIT. I---

I HAVE NO RIGHT TO SAY ANYTHING TO YOU AT ALL.

I SAY WHAT YOU DO AND DON'T HAVE, COWBOY.

* CRACKLING *

* LAUGHING *

* LAUGHING *

* LAUGHING *

YOU'RE SMILING.

IT'S JUST NICE TO BE INSIDE ON A RAINY NIGHT. MAKES YOU THANKFUL.

YES, IT DOES.

WHERE IS YOUR FAMILY, WEBER?

I DON'T HAVE ANY FAMILY TO SPEAK OF, SIR.

......

* CLEARING HIS THROAT *

WEBER'S MOTHER PASSED AWAY WHEN HE WAS FOURTEEN, AND HIS FATHER, WHO WAS A ROUGHNECK ON AN OIL RIG, WAS KILLED IN AN ACCIDENT A YEAR LATER.

WEBER AND HIS OLDER BROTHER SPENCER WERE ALONE AFTER THAT. SPENCER WAS SEVENTEEN WHEN IT HAPPENED.

I SEE.

AND WHERE IS SPENCER NOW?

SPENCER WAS KILLED IN IRAQ WHEN HE WAS TWENTY.

* CRACKLING *

* BURNING *

SINCE I'M THE ONLY ONE LEFT OUTTA MY FAMILY, I HAVE ALL THEIR STUFF IN A STORAGE SPACE IN ABILENE THAT I USED MY BROTHER'S LIFE INSURANCE MONEY FROM THE ARMY TO PAY FOR.

THAT'S GREAT, BUT IF ANYTHING SHOULD HAPPEN TO YOU...

I HAVE THE ADDRESS OF THE STORAGE SPACE AND THE SPARE KEY.

* NODDING *

YOUR SON IS MY EMERGENCY CONTACT IN MY WALLET.

IF I GET TRAMPLED OR SHOT OR GORED OR---

STOP!

* WHOOSH *

SHE GETS IT.

SORRY, MA'AM.

LIFE AS A DRIFTER AND BULL RIDER IS KIND OF UNPREDICTABLE.

OKAY...

I'M GOING TO BED.

HAVE A GOOD NI---

* GROAN *

꾸욱

WHAT?

* DEEP SIGH *

THEY ALL THINK I'M SOME SAD SACK NOW.

WHY'D YOU HAVE TO GO AND TELL'EM THAT I'M A DAMN ORPHAN AND GET ALL MAUDLIN ON ME?

WEBER, I---

OH, WEBER.

* LAUGHING *

하하

OH FOR CRISSAKES, GET OFF ME.

* HUGGING *

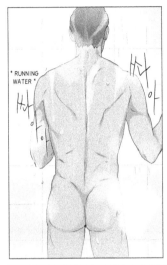

* RUNNING WATER *

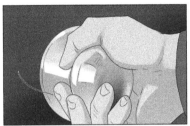

* MOVEMENT *

HEY.

ROSS...

Chapter 11

YOU HEARD ME AND BRETT TALKING EARLIER, DIDN'T YOU?

YES, I DID.

I'M SORRY. THAT WAS RUDE.

I WON'T LIE AND SAY THAT WHEN YOU'RE GONE, I'M NOT GOING TO ASK CYRUS OUT.

BUT FOR NOW, I'LL BACK OFF. I'M LEAVING IN THE MORNING.

I CAN'T COMPETE WITH THE WHOLE ORPHANED COWBOY BULLSHIT.

HE AND CYRUS WOULD FIT TOGETHER.

* DEEP SIGH *

* WHOOSH *

ARE YOU AN IDIOT?

HOW CAN YOU LEAVE A MAN WHO LOOKS LIKE THAT OR WORKS THAT JOB OR HAS THE FINANCIAL PORTFOLIO HE HAS?

YOU KEEP THINKING THAT YOU CAN RIDE OFF AND HE'LL JUST BE HERE WHEN YOU GET BACK EACH TIME, AND THAT'S IDIOTIC.

* SLAM! *

관!

* WHOOSH *

* FLINCH *

YOU DON'T THINK YOU DESERVE HIM, RIGHT? A MAN LIKE YOU, LACKING IN PROSPECTS AND EVERYTHING ELSE, WHERE DO YOU GET OFF EVEN BEING HERE OR---

* SHARP GLANCE *

OH, HEY.

WEB?

ARE YOU COMING TO BED? I'VE BEEN WAITING FOR A LONG TIME.

GRIN

COMIN' RIGHT NOW.

"LOCKING THE DOOR."

THANK YOU.

FOR WHAT?

WANTIN' ME INSTEAD OF THE GUY WHO'S BETTER FOR YOU.

WEBER.

YOU'RE THE ONLY ONE WHO'S GOOD FOR ME.

* FALLING WITH A THUD *

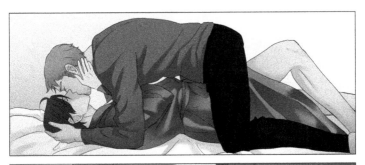

* LICKING *

* SQUEEZING HARD *

* ROLLING *

GOD, I FUCKIN' HATE YOU.

* LEANING DOWN *

CYRUS?

YOU BELONG TO ME. YOU'RE MINE!

WHAT IS SO WRONG WITH LETTING ME STAKE YOU IN A BUSINESS?

DOING WHAT?

I DON'T KNOW. WHATEVER YOU WANT. I COULD SPONSOR YOU.

MY BODY CAN'T RODEO NO MORE. I MAY BE STUPID, BUT I AIN'T SUICIDAL. I'LL FIND A RANCH WHERE I CAN---

I DON'T WANT YOU ON A RANCH SOMEWHERE IN TEXAS! I WANT YOU RIGHT HERE!

THIS WAS WHAT HAD HAPPENED THE LAST TIME, AND I REMEMBERED HIS ULTIMATUM, HOW ANGRY HE'D BEEN, TREMBLING WITH RAGE, FURIOUS AT HIMSELF AND HIS TEARS, LIVID THAT I HAD ANY POWER OVER HIM AT ALL.

* GETS UP *

I SHOULDN'T HAVE COME TO SEE YOU. THIS WAS A MISTAKE.

WEBER.

JUST WHEN THE DAMN THING WAS HEALIN', I SHOW UP AND TEAR OFF THE BANDAGE AND MAKE IT START TO BLEED ALL OVER AGAIN.

WEBER...

* MOVEMENT *

DID YOU EVER THINK THAT THE ONLY THING YOU'RE SUPPOSED TO DO IS JUST LOVE ME?

LOVE...

OH, HE'S SCARED NOW.

* FLOPS DOWN *

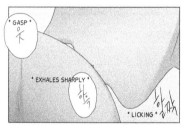

* GASP *

CYRUS.

YES, BABY?

* LICKING *

* FLINCH *

* CLICK *

* SQUEEZING *

I'LL TRUST YOU IF YOU TRUST ME.

* POURING *

WHAT DOES THAT MEAN?

YOU FUCK ME WITHOUT A RUBBER.

* FREEZE *

......

YOU'RE A DOCTOR. I KNOW YOU HAVE SAFE SEX, AND WE'VE NEVER DONE IT TOGETHER WITHOUT ONE, AND I AIN'T NEVER DONE IT WITH NOBODY ELSE WITHOUT ONE.

YOU HEARD ME RIGHT.

IF YOU'RE GONNA COME IN MY ASS, I WANNA FEEL IT. I WANNA BE DRIPPIN' WITH YOU.

* DRIPPING *

* LEAKING *

* SPEECHLESS *

AH...

I'M SORRY. I DIDN'T MEAN TO PRESSURE YOU.

YOU'RE SUCH AN IDIOT!

WEBER, TURN AROUND.

WHAT?

* THROWS THE BOTTLE IN THE AIR *

* INHALES SHARPLY *

* SOB *

SHALLOW BREATH

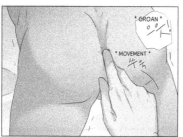

* GROAN *

* MOVEMENT *

HOW CAN YOU BELIEVE...

* GRUNTING *

...THAT I WOULD REFUSE TO FUCK YOU BARE?

THERE'S NO WAY I WON'T DO IT.

* LEAKING *

Chapter 12

YOU OFFER ME YOUR VIRGIN ASSHOLE WITH NOTHING BETWEEN US AT THE SAME TIME YOU'RE MAKING PLANS TO LEAVE ME IN TWO WEEKS?

* GASP *

IS THERE ANYONE ON THE PLANET AS STUPID AS YOU?

ARE YOU LISTENING TO ME?

* GASP *

OH, CYRUS.

* GROAN *

* FINGER PENETRATING *

I HAVE A TEST DONE EVERY SIX MONTHS, WEBER. HOW ABOUT YOU?

* FLINCH *

I HAD A CHECKUP FOUR MONTHS AGO... IT ALL CAME BACK NEGATIVE. I'M...CLEAN.

I'M GONNA ADD A FINGER.

DOES IT FEEL GOOD?

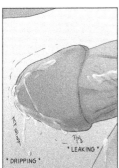

SAY IT!
JUST YOU.
I WILL NEVER HURT YOU.
* MOVEMENT *
I KNOW. I TRUST YOU.
REMEMBER THAT.
* SHOVING HARD *
* MOVEMENT *

* GASP *

* RAMMING IN *

* MOAN *

FIRST I FELT A
BURNING PAIN
LIKE I HAD
NEVER FELT
BEFORE...

* ROCKING *

* RAMMING IN *

* POUNDING HARD *

...BUT SOON
IT BECAME AN
EXQUISITE
THRILL.

* ROCKING *

* GASP *

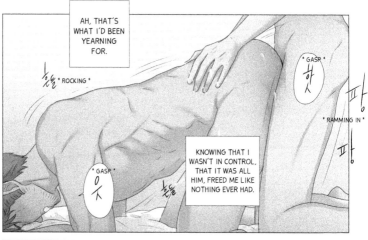

AH, THAT'S WHAT I'D BEEN YEARNING FOR.

* ROCKING *

* GASR *

* RAMMING IN *

* GASR *

KNOWING THAT I WASN'T IN CONTROL, THAT IT WAS ALL HIM, FREED ME LIKE NOTHING EVER HAD.

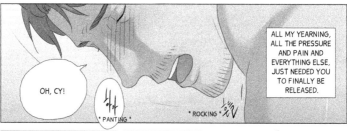

OH, CY!

ALL MY YEARNING, ALL THE PRESSURE AND PAIN AND EVERYTHING ELSE, JUST NEEDED YOU TO FINALLY BE RELEASED.

* PANTING *

* ROCKING *

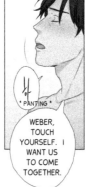

* PANTING *

WEBER, TOUCH YOURSELF. I WANT US TO COME TOGETHER.

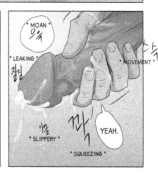

* MOAN *

* LEAKING *

* MOVEMENT *

* SLIPPERY *

YEAH.

* SQUEEZING *

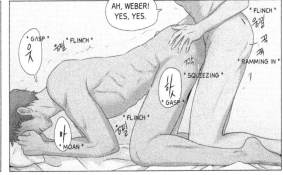

* PANTING *

* EXHALES DEEPLY *

* HOLDING TIGHT *

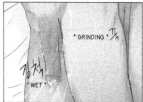

* GRINDING *

* WET *

THE URGE TO GET UP AND RUN AWAY WAS AS POWERFUL AS THE ONE TO ROLL OVER AND PULL CYRUS DOWN INTO MY ARMS.

I WAS TERRIFIED AND SATED AND SORE AND JOYFUL.

WHAT THE HELL?

* RUNNING WATER *

* GRUNT *

* GASP *

* SHIVERING *

MY MUSCLES HURT SO MUCH. I CAN'T MOVE.

HIS EYES, WHICH WERE FILLING WITH TEARS, WERE GORGEOUS.

BECAUSE I LOVE YOU.

BUT.

CYRUS, WHY ARE YOU TELLING ME THIS NOW?

HUSH.

CYRUS.

JUST SAY IT.

WHY? IT WON'T CHANGE NOTHIN'.

I THINK IT WILL CHANGE EVERYTHING. I NEED TO HEAR IT ALREADY.

I LOVE YOU, WEBER YATES SO MUCH, SO COMPLETELY

JESUS CHRIST, CY. YOU KNOW I LOVE YOU! THAT'S NOT THE PROBLEM, IS IT? IT'S NEVER BEEN THE PROBLEM WITH US.

Chapter 13

STRETCHING

GRUNT

MAY i JOIN YOU?

YES, MA'AM.

I REALLY WOULD LIKE YOU TO CALL ME RACHEL.

OKAY, RACHEL.

CYRUS IS HEAD OVER HEELS IN LOVE WITH YOU, AND MY GIRLS ARE TOO.

MY HUSBAND PROBABLY WON'T BE ABLE TO LOOK YOU IN THE EYES THIS MORNING.

WHY?

YOU KNOW WHY.

MY MOTHER-IN-LAW CAME TO OUR ROOM LAST NIGHT TO REAM HIM OUT.

RUNNING

SHIT, NOW I FEEL BAD.

YOU SHOULDN'T.

I'VE KNOWN CYRUS FOR OVER TEN YEARS, AND IT'S THE FIRST TIME I'VE SEEN HIM THIS WAY. HE'S NEVER BEEN ANYTHING BUT LOGICAL AND PRACTICAL AND, HONESTLY, MORE THAN A LITTLE COLD.

......

COME ON, I KNOW A GOOD TRAIL.

OKAY.

* RUNNING

I DON'T UNDERSTAND WHAT YOU WERE TRYIN' TO SAY ABOUT CYRUS BEFORE.

AH.

CYRUS IS DIFFERENT. HE'S COMPLETELY CHANGED WHEN YOU'RE AROUND.

HOW DO YA MEAN?

THAT GUY YESTERDAY--- HAPPY, SMILING, WARM GUY--- I'VE NEVER MET HIM BEFORE.

CYRUS...?

* FREEZING *

I'M NOT SAYING THAT HE DOESN'T LOVE HIS FAMILY, BUT HE NEVER SMILES AND HE'S ALWAYS SO SERIOUS. HE'S JUST SO HARSH AND SO LOST IN HIS OWN HEAD SOMETIMES.

WHEN THERE'S A FAMILY GATHERING, WE ALL LOOK FORWARD TO HIM LEAVING SO THE REST OF US CAN RELAX AND LAUGH AND JUST HAVE FUN ONCE HE'S GONE.

THAT MAKES NO SENSE...

. . . . . .

DO YOU GET WHAT I'M SAYING?

NO, I TRULY DO NOT.

DON'T GET ME WRONG. IF I HAD A BRAIN TUMOR, CYRUS IS THE GUY I WOULD GO TO IN A HEARTBEAT. BUT THE FACE HE MAKES WHEN HE'S STARING AT YOU, THE WAY HE CAN'T KEEP HIS HANDS OFF YOU... I REALLY HAD NO IDEA HE HAD THAT IN HIM.

CAROLYN SAID BEING WITH YOU GUYS AT HIS HOUSE WAS ABSOLUTELY SURREAL.

THAT'S BECAUSE YOU'VE NEVER SEEN THE CYRUS I'M TALKING ABOUT.

LET'S KEEP RUNNING.

THANK YOU FOR RUNNING WITH MY WIFE.

* FAST MOVEMENT *

OH.

IT WAS MY PLEASURE.

I HURT MY KNEE SO I CAN'T GO WITH HER ANYMORE. THANK YOU.

YOU'RE WELCOME.

AND...I WAS TRYING TO GET MY BROTHER A LIFE, BUT I WAS A DICK TO YOU. I APOLOGIZE.

* HESITANT *

WE'RE GOOD. DON'T STRAIN NOTHIN'.

* SUDDENLY *

DID YOU SLEEP WELL, COWBOY?

HERE.

THANK YOU, SIR.

IT'S EXHAUSTING TO PLAY WITH THE KIDS, HUH?

NO, SIR. THEY JUST HAVE A LOT OF ENERGY, WHICH IS GREAT.

* POURING RAIN *

* POURING RAIN *

WEBER, I EXPECT TO SEE YOU FOR CHRISTMAS. DON'T LEAVE BEFORE THEN.

I'LL TRY TO BE THERE.

WE WOULD ALL REALLY LIKE TO SEE MORE OF YOU.

THANK YOU, MR. BENNING.

CALL ME OWEN.

YESSIR.

I WOULD LOVE TO, SIR, BUT I'M A RANCH HAND AND IT WOULD BE DIFFICULT TO FIND A JOB IN SAN FRANCISCO.

YES, I KNOW.

DO YOU CARE FOR HIM THE SAME WAY AS HE SO OBVIOUSLY CARES FOR YOU?

NODDING

OF COURSE. THAT AIN'T NEVER BEEN OUR PROBLEM.

GOOD.

DAD.

GLANCE

YOUR BELOVED PACK IS PLAYING. GET IN HERE IF YOU DON'T WANT TO MISS IT.

YOU SEE THAT? I HAD NO IDEA HE EVEN KNEW GREEN BAY WAS MY TEAM.

PAT

I'LL BE RIGHT IN.

* SITTING DOWN *

WHY ARE YOU SMILING?

YOU LOOK REALLY COMFORTABLE IN MY PARENTS' HOME.

YEAH, IT FEELS GOOD TO BE HERE.

CAN I HAVE THAT KISS NOW?

* PUTS HIS HAND DOWN *

OH HELL NO. YOU DIDN'T WANT IT EARLIER.

YOU WERE DISGUSTING EARLIER, BUT NOW YOU'RE ALL CLEAN AND YOU SMELL GOOD.

AND YOU---

* SUDDEN MOVEMENT *

* MOAN *

* KISSING *

* MOAN *

* SIGH OF PLEASURE *

WE SHOULD GO BACK IN.

* KISSING *

YEAH, LET'S GO.

* MOAN *

Chapter 14

THE KIDS LEFT?

YES, THEY JUST DID.

* CLATTERING *

THEY DIDN'T WANT TO GO HOME. THEY WANTED TO SLEEP WITH YOU. MY SISTER WAS ALMOST BEGGING THEM TO GET IN THE CAR.

REALLY? WELL DONE. THANK YOU FOR COOKING TONIGHT.

SEEMS LIKE MY FAMILY LOVED YOU.

* HOLDING TIGHT *

REALLY?

MY DAD AND MOM LOVED YOU. EVEN BRETT, THE KIDS, AND RACHEL SEEMED TO LOVE YOU.

* KISS *

LIKE YOU LOVE ME?

I WANT TO TELL EVERYONE THAT YOU'RE MINE. I WANT TO KEEP YOU AND PUT A RING ON YOUR FINGER AND COME HOME EVERY NIGHT TO YOUR FACE LOOKING AT ME LIKE I'M AN IDIOT.

I NEVER LOOK AT YOU LIKE YOU'RE AN---

WEBER.

* SCREECHING *

YEAH, YOU DO. WHEN I'VE DONE SOMETHING PARTICULARLY STUPID, YOU DO.

WELL, OF COURSE THEN, BUT---

STOP CHANGING THE SUBJECT. YOU FOCUSING ON ONE PA WHAT I SAID TO AVO REST. LAST TIME YOU I REALLY THOUGHT I GONNA DIE.

*MOVEMENT *

* DEEP SIGH *

CYRUS, WHEN I CALLED YOU FROM THE BUS TERMINAL, WHY DIDN'T YOU JUST TELL ME TO GO ON AND NOT STOP TO SEE YOU?

BECAUSE I THOUGHT ONE OF THESE DAYS YOU WERE GOING TO LET ME LOVE YOU.

I THOUGHT WHEN THAT DAY WOULD COME, YOU'D STOP LEAVING ME AND STAY BY MY SIDE.

......

GRINDING

NO!

WHAT NO?

I'M HAVING A SERIOUS DISCUSSION WITH YOU! DO NOT GIMME THAT LOOK LIKE YOU WANT TO FUCK ME BECAUSE IT WON'T WORK.

LIFT

STARTLED

NEVER IN MY LIFE HAD I BEEN THE HOT GUY OR THE SEXY GUY, BUT I HAD A DRUGGING EFFECT ON CYRUS BENNING. I MELTED HIM, AND HE DID THE SAME TO ME.

* MOAN *

HE HAS THE SAME EFFECT ON ME.

I...YOU CAN KEEP TOUCHING ME, WEB, BUT MAKE NO MISTAKE, I'M GOING WITH YOU WHEN YOU LEAVE. I WON'T LIVE WITHOUT YOU ANYMORE, I CAN'T.

* MOVEMENT *

WHY WOULD I ARGUE WITH HIM? WELL, I WOULD, BUT LATER... MUCH LATER.

* JEANS RUSTLING *

* CLINKING *

THERE ARE MORE URGENT MATTERS RIGHT NOW.

* WHOOSH *

* HOARSE MOAN *

NOW IT'S MY TURN TO FILL YOU UP, DR. BENNING.

DON'T USE A RUBBER.

WHAT?

OH GOD, WEBER, MOVE! GET THE FUCKING LUBE!

* SHIVERING *

WEBER!

* SHAKING *

I WANNA FEEL YOUR HEART BEATING.

NO, STAY INSIDE. I NEED...CLOSER.

NO ONE EVER WANTED ME THE WAY HE DID.

I WONDERED IF PLANNING ON LEAVING MADE ME THE STUPIDEST MAN ON THE PLANET.

Chapter 15

HERE IS THE PROBLEM: CYRUS LIKES ME BECAUSE I'M A BULL RIDER AND A COWBOY, BUT...

...IF I WANT TO STAY BY HIS SIDE, I'LL HAVE TO LEARN TO DO SOMETHING ELSE AND WON'T BE ABLE TO SATISFY CYRUS'S ROMANTIC FANTASIES.

IF HE LEAVES HIS LIFE TO FOLLOW ME, HE WOULD HATE ME FOR WHAT I LET HIM GIVE UP.

SO YEAH, WHEN THE TIME COMES, I'LL LEAVE. ONCE I'M SETTLED SOMEWHERE, CYRUS WILL COME AND VISIT ME. AS LONG AS NO OTHER MAN COMES TO CLAIM HIM...

BUT I CAN'T EXPECT CYRUS TO REMAIN UNCLAIMED. THAT IS JUST PLAIN STUPID.

* SNICKERING. *

YOU'VE BEEN WAITING FOR A WHILE, HUH?

SORRY IT TOOK ME SO LONG TO GET DOWN HERE.

NO, I KNOW YOU'RE BUSY.

HERE, YOUR LAPTOP.

THANK YOU FOR BRINGING IT TO ME.

I HAVE A FUNDRAISER TO GO TO TONIGHT THAT I COMPLETELY BLANKED ON. YOU WANT TO GO WITH ME?

ISN'T IT THE EVENT YOU TALKED ABOUT SOME TIME AGO?

NO, THAT'S THE ANNUAL CHRISTMAS PARTY. THERE ARE A FEW OTHERS AS WELL, BUT THIS ONE NEVER EVEN MADE IT INTO MY CALENDAR.

I SEE.

SO? I WANT YOU TO GO WITH ME.

OH HELL NO, DOC. I WON'T GO TO SLEEP AND I'LL WAIT UP FOR YA.

COME WITH ME, WEBER.

NOT IF YA PAID ME.

* WHINING *

YOU'RE JUST---

CAROLYN, THE BOYS, AND ME ARE GOING TO MAKE STROGANOFF FOR DINNER.

OH, THAT SOUNDS SO GOOD. SAVE ME SOME.

WE'LL TRY.

GET HOME SOON AS YOU CAN.

* TAP *

I GOTTA GO.

NO, STAY AND HAVE LUNCH WITH ME.

THE KIDS WILL BE HERE SOON, AND WE'RE GOIN' TO THE WHARF TO GET US SOME CLAM CHOWDER. I HEARD THERE'S A GREAT RESTAURANT ON THE WAY TO MICAH'S APPOINTMENT WITH HIS SHRINK.

KIDS DON'T EAT CLAM CHOWDER.

YOU WANNA BET?

I'M NOT GOING TO BET YOU. JUST... THEY WON'T EAT IT.

MAYBE THEY'LL EAT IT ALL.

* SHAKING HIS HEAD *

* MOVEMENT *

IF THE BOYS EAT CLAM CHOWDER, MY ASS IS YOURS WHEN I GET HOME FROM THE FUNDRAISER. IF THEY DON'T, YOURS BELONGS TO ME.

* SCOFFING *

OH, YOU'RE SO UNDER ME THE SECOND YOU WALK IN THE DOOR.

* FLUSHED *

DR. BENNING?

* WHOOSH *

COULD I GET AN INTRODUCTION?

...UM.

THE BOYS WILL BE WAITING FOR ME. I SHOULD GO.

NO.

* WHOOSH *

WEBER, THIS IS OUR CHIEF OF SURGERY, DR. HAROLD SWAN. CHIEF, THIS IS MY BOYFRIEND, WEBER YATES.

* SHRUG *

WEBER, IT'S VERY GOOD TO MEET YOU. IT'S SUCH A PLEASURE.

THANK YOU.

* BUZZING *

YOUR BOYFRIEND?

THAT'S WHAT YOU ARE.

WE'RE MORE THAN FRIENDS, BUT WE'RE NOT PARTNERS LIVING UNDER THE SAME ROOF. EVEN THOUGH I WOULD LIKE FOR US TO LIVE TOGETHER. WOULD "LOVER" HAVE BEEN BETTER?

HELL NO. THEY SURPRISED ME BY COMING AT US ALL AT ONCE.

* BUZZING *

THEY ALL KNOW I'M GAY, BUT I WOULD NEVER DATE ANYONE AT THIS HOSPITAL OR ASSOCIATED WITH THIS HOSPITAL.

BECAUSE DATING A COLLEAGUE COULD BECOME A PROBLEM?

AMONG OTHER THINGS, YES. I DON'T BRING DATES HERE AND NO ONE COMES TO PICK ME UP AT THE HOSPITAL, SO YOU'RE KIND OF A NOVELTY FOR THEM.

DON'T YOU HAVE FRIENDS HERE?

I HAVE COLLEAGUES.

MOST OF MY GOOD FRIENDS HAVE PRIVATE PRACTICES, AND MY BEST FRIENDS AREN'T DOCTORS.

THEY'RE THE GUYS WHO CAME ALONG WITH YOU ON THE TRIP TO TEXAS, HUH? THE DENTIST, THE LAWYER AND THE REAL ESTATE GUY?

* BUZZING *

YES. THOUGH HE'S NOT IN REAL ESTATE---HE'S A LAND DEVELOPER.

DO YOU STILL SEE THEM?

WE'RE SUPPOSED TO TAKE A TRIP TO CANCUN IN FEBRUARY.

I'M SURE YOU'LL HAVE A GREAT TIME.

* BUZZING *

I'D RATHER STAY HOME.

* BUZZING *

I WON'T BE HERE.

YOU NEVER KNOW.

BUT I'VE ALREADY MADE UP MY MIND.

THE CLAM CHOWDER WAS REALLY GOOD.

YOU ALL LIKED IT?

YES!

LOVED IT!

* SEAGULLS *

I SHOULD CALL UNCLE CYRUS TO MAKE HIM JEALOUS.

ME TOO!

YOU ALREADY HAVE A CELL PHONE?

YES, MOM WAS ALWAYS WORRYING SO SHE BOUGHT ME ONE.

UNCLE CYRUS? THIS IS TRISTAN.

HEY! DID YOU LIKE THE CLAM CHOWDER?

YES!

IT WAS DELICIOUS. WE ATE IT ALL.

THAT'S AWESOME. I LOVE IT WHEN YOU GUYS EAT.

* VROOM *

* CLEARING HIS THROAT *

I HEARD THAT, WEBER. ASS.

YOURS.

* VROOM *

I WAS EXPECTING AN OFFICE BUT...

* DONKEY *

* COW *

* FLAPPING *

...THIS IS NOT SO BAD.

* DUCK *

* CHICKEN *

* FLAPPING *

* CHICK *

* ROOSTER *

* SWAYING *

HEH.

* ELECTRONIC SOUNDS *

YOU'RE A REAL COWBOY?

NOT ANYMORE.

MICAH SAYS YOU ARE.

* RUNNING *

* BOWING *

I AM DR. ERIN WATASE.

I'M WEBER. I'M WATCHING OVER THE KIDS.

I HEARD A LOT ABOUT YOU.

MICAH TALKED ABOUT ME?

HE DID THROUGH HIS DRAWINGS.

AH. I SEE.

GO PLAY WITH YOUR BROTHERS.

* NOD *

* SCREECHING *

* RUNNING *

I'M GLAD TO SEE THE WORTHLESS NANNY IS GONE AND YOU'RE HERE.

ONLY FOR A COUPLE WEEKS.

ARE YOU CERTAIN?

WHY WOULD YOU ASK THAT?

* GRIN *

씨익

ME?

WELL, BECAUSE MICAH LIKES YOU A LOT.

YES, HE FEELS SAFE WHEN YOU'RE AROUND.

HE BELIEVES YOU WON'T GET HURT OR LEAVE HIM.

끄덕

* NOD *

HOW WOULD YOU KNOW THAT?

WHEN I ASKED HIM TO DRAW SOMETHING THAT REPRESENTED YOU, HE DREW A MOUNTAIN.

A MOUNTAIN...

OF COURSE HE WOULD. I'M A LOT BIGGER THAN HIM.

YOU DON'T SEEM PLEASED. WHAT'S WRONG WITH BEING A MOUNTAIN?

IT'S SO BORING. I COULDN'T BE A MUSTANG OR A CHEETAH?

* SHRUG *

* LAUGHING SOFTLY *

A MOUNTAIN IS A VERY GOOD THING, MR. YATES.

WEBER. IF YOU WOULD PLEASE CALL ME BY MY GIVEN NAME, I WOULD BE MUCH OBLIGED.

OH!

"OBLIGED." I HAVEN'T HEARD THAT WORD IN YEARS.

Chapter 16

A MOUNTAIN IS PRECISELY WHAT MICAH NEEDS RIGHT NOW. HIS GRANDMOTHER AND HIS FATHER JUST DISAPPEARED FROM HIS LIFE.

RIGHT NOW, MICAH THINKS THAT HIS GRANDMA AND HIS FATHER ABANDONED HIM.

CHANGE IS NOT GOOD FOR HIM. HE NEEDS A FOUNDATION.

HE HAS HIS MOTHER.

BUT HE'S A BIG BOY.

MICAH'S MOTHER DOES NOT HAVE TIME TO SIT AND HUG HIM.

HE'S SIX. SIX IS NOT BIG. SIX NEEDS TO BE LOVED ON VERY HARD.

CAROLYN IS GIVING HIM ALL HER LOVE.

* NOD *

AGREED. SHE'S DOING THE BEST SHE CAN TO FIRST NAVIGATE HER OWN LOSS AND THEN THAT OF HER CHILDREN.

BUT SHE WAKES UP EACH DAY WITH THREE BOYS WHO REQUIRE HER FULL ATTENTION, WHICH IS A DAUNTING TASK.

YES, YOU'RE RIGHT.

CAROLYN AND THE BOYS NEED HELP. KIDS NEED BOTH PARENTS TO SUPPORT THEM PROPERLY.

A MAN AND A WOMAN?

THAT'S ONE OF MANY GOOD COMBINATIONS. BUT I LIKE TWO MEN, TWO WOMEN, OR GRANDPARENTS JUST AS WELL. IT DOESN'T MATTER TO ME. AND I'M NOT SAYING THAT SINGLE PARENTS AREN'T ASTOUNDING---I WAS ONE, FOR GOODNESS SAKES---BUT HELP, RELIEF OF SOME KIND, SOME FORM, IS NEEDED.

* WHOOSH *

SURE. THAT'S WHY SHE'LL GET HERSELF A FULL-TIME NANNY AFTER I LEAVE.

WEBER, ALL CHILDREN NEED A ROLE MODEL.

THEY DON'T NEED A MIRACLE WORKER, BUT SIMPLY SOMEONE TO ASK THEM HOW THEIR DAY WAS, TO PACK THEIR LUNCH,

AND SING ALONG TO THE RADIO IN THE CAR.

AND THERE IS SOMETHING YOU MUST NOT FORGET.

THE DAY THEIR NANNY AND THEIR FATHER WALKED OUT, YOU WALKED IN.

...

CLOSE A DOOR; OPEN A WINDOW. DO YOU UNDERSTAND?

* SHRUG *

NOT REALLY.

THESE CHILDREN ARE SCARRED BY THEIR FATHER'S LEAVING. RIGHT NOW, WITH HIS ABSENCE, THE SPACE BETWEEN THEM LOOMS WIDER AND WIDER.

SO NOW WE'VE TAUGHT CHILDREN TO FEAR BEING ABANDONED, AND SO AS ADULTS THEY EITHER PUSH PEOPLE AWAY SO AS NOT TO BE HURT, OR HOLD THEM TOO TIGHT AND SUFFOCATE THEM.

THAT SEEMS MUCH TOO SIMPLE TO ME.

AND MAYBE IT IS. MAYBE THIS WON'T AFFECT THEM AT ALL. WHAT ARE YOUR THOUGHTS?

* SHAKING HIS HEAD *

I HAVE NO IDEA.

WE ALL CARRY WHAT WE'VE LEARNED AND EXPERIENCED WITH US THROUGHOUT OUR LIFE.

* NOD *

THEIR FATHER'S DISAPPEARANCE WILL NOT BE EASILY FORGOTTEN. PHILLIP MIGHT NOT HOLD ON TO HIS FATHER'S DISAPPEARANCE BECAUSE HE'S STILL YOUNG, BUT...

...I'M NOT SO SURE ABOUT THE OTHER TWO. THEY ARE OLD ENOUGH TO WONDER WHO WILL BE THE NEXT TO LEAVE THEM.

IT'LL BE ME. I'M FIXIN' TO LEAVE IN A COUPLE WEEKS, RIGHT AFTER NEW YEAR'S.

THAT WON'T WORK.

PARDON?

* SHAKING HER HEAD *

MICAH IS BONDED WITH YOU. THANKS TO YOU, HE MIGHT EVEN TALK FAIRLY SOON.

HE SO WANTED TO TELL ME ABOUT YOU TODAY. HE COULDN'T DRAW FAST ENOUGH. HE WANTED TO EXPRESS SO MANY THINGS.

WHEN I WAS DELIBERATELY OBTUSE, HE WAS VERY IRRITATED WITH ME. I THINK HE THOUGHT I WAS SMARTER.

YOU TRICKED HIM.

* NOD *

I HAVE TO FIND A WAY TO MAKE HIM TALK BEFORE HE CLOSES OFF COMPLETELY. SHOCKING HIM OR PUTTING HIM IN A SITUATION WHERE SOMEONE ELSE COULD BE HURT IF HE DIDN'T USE HIS VOICE---THAT'S ALL SHIT, YOU KNOW?

I CAN'T BELIEVE YOU SAID "SHIT."

OUR WORK IS IMPORTANT, SO WE MUST NOT USE SHITTY METHODS.

* GRIN *

TRISTAN AND MICAH LOOK AT Y○ WITH EYES FULL C WANT AND HOPE WHATEVER YOU D○ DON'T KILL IT BECA I'LL HAVE TO KIL YOU.

IT DOESN'T MAKE SENSE. YOU'RE SAYING THAT I'M RESPONSIBLE FOR THE PSYCHE OF THESE BOYS?

* NOD *

EXACTLY.

YOU DIDN'T THINK I KNEW THE WORD "PSYCHE", DIDJA?

* LAUGHING OUT LOUD *

* STARTLED *

* PAT *

YOU'RE A FUNNY MAN.

* OH *

* ENGROSSED *

* ELECTRONIC SOUNDS *

* CLATTERING *

WEBER!

* HURRIEDLY *

I'M SORRY TO BE SO LATE.

NO PROBLEM, YOU CALLED ME BEFOREHAND TO LET ME KNOW.

THERE WAS SO MUCH WORK I COULDN'T LEAVE THE OFFICE. SORRY.

THE BOYS ARE ALREADY FED AND SHOWERED AND NOW THEY'RE PLAYING. THEY'RE IN THEIR PAJAMAS.

MOM!

HEY.

* SUDDEN MOVEMENT *

* SWEET SMILE *

DID YOU EAT WELL?

YES!

AWESOME.

* SOB *

* SOBBING *

* SOB *

CAROLYN.

ARE YOU CRYING, MOM?

* PATTING WITH CARE *

WEBER.

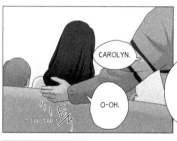

CAROLYN.

O-OH.

* TAP TAP *

OF COURSE.
IT LOOKS
LIKE HIM.

* NOD *

* SITTING WITH
A THUD *

* EYES WELLING
WITH TEARS *

EARLIER, DOCTOR
ERIN SAID THAT HE WAS
FIXIN' TO TALK SOON.

YOU SHOULD START HEARIN' SOME WORDS SPRINKLED IN WITH HIS NODS. BUT YOU SHOULDN'T MAKE IT A BIG DEAL OR ELSE HE'LL BE THINKIN' HE'S DIFFERENT.

SO JUST, WHEN HE TALKS TO YOU, TALK BACK.

* DEEP SIGH *

IF YOU HEARD WHAT I TOLD YOU, TRY SAYING "YES, I HEARD YOU, WEBER."

ONE FUCKING DAY.

PARDON?

* SHALLOW BREATH *

* PAT *

...

YES, I HEARD YOU, WEBER.

* SOB *

THEY WERE WITH YOU ONE FUCKING DAY, AND THEY'RE ALREADY CHANGING.

MICAH IS FEELING SO GROUNDED THAT HE WANTS TO START TALKING AGAIN, AND ALL THREE OF THEM LOOK HAPPY AND CONTENT LIKE I HAVEN'T SEEN THEM IN MONTHS.

I DON'T KNOW WHAT'S HAPPENING EITHER. APPARENTLY MICAH TOLD DOCTOR ERIN THAT I WAS A MOUNTAIN.

WHAT?

NEVER MIND. ARE YOU HUNGRY? WE MADE STROGANOFF.

OH MY!

어머

I GET DINNER TOO?

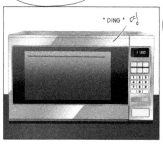

* DING *

삐!

HERE.

* MOVEMENT *

척

THANK YOU.

WEBER, YOU TAKE BETTER CARE OF MY BOYS THAN MY HUSBAND DID, AND YOU CARE MORE ABOUT ME.

NEXT TIME YOU MEET A MAN, YOU SHOULD MAKE SURE HE'S SWEET ON ALL OF YOU.

* NOD *

THAT'S REAL SAD.

I'LL DO THAT.

TOMORROW I'M SUPPOSED TO GO TO A CHRISTMAS PARTY AND WE'RE ALL BRINGING OUR CHILDREN. SOME PEOPLE BRING THEIR NANNIES. WOULD YOU CONSIDER GOING WITH ME?

SURELY. I'D LOVE TO BE THE NANNY.

I WOULD LOVE IT TOO. PERMANENTLY.

FOR NOW, EAT YOUR DINNER.

ALL RIGHT. THANK YOU.

Chapter 17

I'M BACK.

HOW WAS THE PARTY?

SAME AS ALWAYS.

WHAT'S WITH YOU?

I MISSED YOU.

* SHARP INTAKE OF BREATH *

* KISSING *

* MOAN *

* SIGH OF PLEASURE *

* MOAN *

* PULLING BACK *

WHY ARE YOU STOPPING?

GO CHANGE. THAT TUXEDO COSTS MORE THAN WHAT I GOT IN THE WORLD.

DAMN IT.

* RISING QUICKLY *

* QUIET *

* FOOTSTEPS *

ARE YOU HUNGRY?

WHY? IS THERE ACTUALLY STROGANOFF LEFT?

THERE WAS SOME LEFT, BUT CAROLYN WAS HUNGRY. SHE ATE HER PLATE AND YOURS.

TERRIFIC. SO WHAT, THEN?

ARE YOU GONNA COOK DINNER FOR ME?

SHOULD I?

I'M KIDDING.

* SITTING WITH A THUD *

PUT YOUR FEET UP HERE.

SO GOOD.

* MASSAGE *

* SQUEEZING *

* MOAN *

* PURR *

* MOAN *

* PURRING *

YOU SOUND LIKE YOU'RE GONNA COME.

OF COURSE. DO YOU KNOW HOW LONG IT'S BEEN SINCE SOMEONE RUBBED MY FEET?

* MASSAGE *

* SQUEEZING *

HOW LONG?

SINCE THE LAST TIME YOU DID IT.

* GROAN *

* SQUEEZING *

* MOANING *

YOU KNOW THAT SONG BY THE EAGLES. ABOUT A COWBOY WHO'S WANDERING.

YOU LOVE THE "DESPERADO" GUY, HUH?

WHAT ARE YOU TALKING ABOUT?

I KNOW THE SONG. I JUST DON'T UNDERSTAND THE REFERENCE.

LIKE A COWBOY.

YOU THINK I ONLY LOVE YOU BECAUSE YOU'RE A BULL RIDER?

* RISING QUICKLY *

I DON'T KNOW...

JESUS, WEBER! I DID NOT FALL IN LOVE WITH YOU BECAUSE YOU'RE A COWBOY.

BUT YOU CALL ME "COWBOY" ALL THE TIME.

THAT'S JUST A NICKNAME. I'LL STOP CALLING YOU THAT.

GOD, I HAD NO IDEA YOU THOUGHT SOMETHING SO STUPID.

* RUBBING *

* PURRING *

* SQUEEZING *

* MASSAGE *

I FELL IN LOVE WITH YOU. WITH THE GUY WHO STARTED RUBBING MY FEET AS SOON AS I GOT HOME. I DIDN'T FALL IN LOVE WITH A COWBOY OR A BULL RIDER.

FUCK.

* MASSAGING *

MAN, I HAD NO IDEA YOU WERE SUCH A SUCKER FOR A FOOT RUB.

ONLY FROM YOU, COWBOY. I MEAN, WEB.

IT'S OKAY. YOU CAN CALL ME COWBOY NOW THAT I KNOW IT DON'T MEAN NOTHIN'.

* MASSAGE *

JUST BELIEVE ME, WEBER.

* WHINE *

THE JOB YOU DO DOESN'T MEAN ANYTHING TO ME. YOU CAN DO WHATEVER YOU WANT.

YEAH, BUT---

YOU SHOULD STOP CARING WHAT STRANGERS THINK. DON'T WORRY ABOUT WHAT PEOPLE I KNOW THINK, OR WHAT PEOPLE YOU KNOW THINK. WHAT REALLY MATTERS IS THAT WHAT YOU DO MAKES YOU HAPPY.

BUT THERE HAS TO BE RESPECT.

WHAT RESPECT? ME RESPECTING YOU?

JESUS, WEBER.

I RESPECT YOU MORE THAN ANYONE ELSE I KNOW. YOU'VE DONE EVERYTHING YOU WANTED YOUR WAY.

YOU WENT FOR YOUR DREAM INSTEAD OF JUST SITTING ON YOUR ASS AND TALKING ABOUT IT.

YEAH.

BUT I DIDN'T MAKE IT. I AIN'T A PROFESSIONAL BULL RIDER.

BUT YOU TRIED.

MOST PEOPLE NEVER EVEN HAVE THE BALLS TO TRY.

MOVEMENT

I WILL NEVER, EVER GET TIRED OF YOU.

MOVING

I HAVE NO DESIRE TO WATCH YOU RIDE OFF INTO THE SUNSET. I WANT YOU HERE, AT HOME, EVERY NIGHT, WAITING FOR ME TO GET HERE. DO YOU HAVE ANY IDEA HOW BADLY I WANTED TO LEAVE THAT FUNDRAISER SO I COULD GET BACK TO YOU?

* SQUEEZING TIGHT *

* SIGH OF PLEASURE *

* KISSING *

* SQUEEZING *

WHAT IS IT?

GET UP.

WHAT? WHY?

GET UP.

* STANDING UP *

GO CHANGE INTO YOUR PAJAMAS AND GET IN BED.

WHAT? NO, I WANT---

JUST GO DO IT. I'LL BE RIGHT HERE.

...OKAY.

* CLOSING THE DOOR *

WEBER.

GET IN BED.

* MOVEMENT *

WHY DON'T YOU WANT ME?

* SHEETS RUSTLING *

IDIOT. I ALWAYS WANT YOU.

BUT WE'RE BOTH BEING IDIOTS.

* CHUCKLING *

YOU THINK IF YOU DON'T COME HOME AND FUCK ME THAT I'M GONNA LOSE INTEREST IN YOU. AND I THINK IF I AIN'T RIDING BULLS NO MORE THAT YOU WON'T WANT NOTHIN' TO DO WITH ME.

WE'RE BOTH GROWN MEN AND YET WE'RE THINKING SUCH FOOLISH THINGS. THAT'S KIND OF PATHETIC.

ALL I WANT IS FOR YOU TO REALIZE THAT WHAT YOU DO DOESN'T DICTATE THE KIND OF MAN YOU ARE. WHAT YOU DO AND WHO YOU ARE, ARE TWO SEPARATE THINGS.

NOT NECESSARILY... BUT I'VE ALWAYS THOUGHT THAT IF I WASN'T WILD, YOU WOULDN'T WANT ME. I THOUGHT YOU HAD AN IDEA OF ME IN YOUR MIND THAT I HAD TO FULFILL.

WEBER, I DON'T GIVE A SHIT WHAT YOU DO. I DON'T NEED A COWBOY OR---

A PRINCE?

...YES. I DON'T CARE.

WEBER.

NO ONE MAKES ME LAUGH LIKE YOU DO, AND NO ONE GETS ME LIKE YOU DO.

* MOVEMENT *

I TOOK ONE LOOK AT YOU AND THREW CAUTION TO THE WIND. I CAN'T TELL YOU HOW MANY TIMES I CURSED THAT DECISION...

APPARENTLY, THE SECOND I SAW YOU, I FELL IN LOVE WITH THE ONE MAN I CAN'T HAVE.

JESUS, WEBER, DO YOU REALIZE YOU SIGH LIKE YOU'RE COMING HOME EVERY TIME YOU KISS ME?

SIGH

MOAN

NO, I DIDN'T...

KISSING

I THOUGHT WE WEREN'T GOING TO MAKE LOVE?

DON'T TEASE ME. I CAN'T HELP IT. I'LL MISS BEING IN BED WITH YOU WHEN I'M GONE.

LIKE I'M GOING TO LET YOU GO.

Chapter 18

* LAUGHING *

NOISY

* NOISY *

* SQUEAL *

* LAUGHING *

YOU'RE CAROLYN'S NANNY?

YES, I AM.

IT MUST BE HARD TO TAKE CARE OF THREE BOYS.

WELL, I HAVE THREE TIMES AS MUCH CUTENESS TO DEAL WITH.

HAHA, YOU'RE SO POSITIVE.

* CAR ENGINE *

WAS I?

I HAD TO TELL THREE OF THE WOMEN WHO WORK WITH ME THAT I WAS PAYING YOU VERY WELL AND THAT YOU DID NOT WANT TO LEAVE MY EMPLOYMENT.

* SLEEPING *

DID YOU, NOW?

WEBER, YOU WERE THE BELLE OF THE BALL.

YEAH.

OH MY!

* HICCUP *

* LAUGHING *

GOD, YOU'RE CUTE WHEN YOU'RE DRUNK.

WEBER YATES, I WISH YOU LIKED GIRLS.

AND I WISH YOU COULD HAVE MET MY BROTHER. I'M SURE YOU WOULD HAVE LIKED EACH OTHER.

* SCOFFING *

* BEEP *

VERY FUNNY.

YOU NEEDED A PHONE NOW THAT YOU'VE GOT THE KIDS WITH YOU. AND YOU MIGHT NEED TO CALL ME SOMETIMES TOO.

THIS ONE'S TOO FANCY.

I'LL SHOW YOU ALL THE COOL STUFF IT CAN DO LATER.

ALL RIGHT.

ARE YOU MAD?

JUST THAT I WENT OUT DRINKING WITHOUT YOU.

YOU'RE A BIG BOY. YOU CAN DO AS YOU PLEASE.

WHY WOULD I BE MAD?

NO, I KNOW.

* SLIDING *

......

WHAT'S WRONG? DID YOU HAVE A BAD DAY?

* WAGGING *

WHAT MAKES YOU ASK THAT?

YOU'RE NOT A BIG DRINKER. THERE HAS TO BE A REASON FOR YOU TO DO THAT ON A WHIM.

* BUZZING *

* BUSTLING *

...I HAD A LONG, SHITTY DAY. I LOST A PATIENT.

* LONG SIGH *

I SEE.

SHE WAS A NICE PERSON. SHE WAS A NICE MOTHER, A NICE GRANDMOTHER, AND SHE DIED RIGHT BEFORE CHRISTMAS.

AND DID YOU TELL YOUR FRIENDS THAT?

NO, THAT'S NOT SOMETHING WE DO. WE DON'T SIT AROUND AND SHARE OUR FEELINGS. THAT'S WHAT MY BOYFRIEND IS FOR.

...I SEE.

* SQUEEZING *

THAT'S WHAT YOU'RE FOR.

I MEAN, I TOLD THEM I HAD A FUCKED-UP DAY, AND THEY JUST TOLD ME TO DRINK AND FEEL BETTER.

YOU SHOULD HAVE JUST COME ON HOME.

I KNOW THAT!

* SUDDENLY *

WHY ARE YOU YELLIN'?

BECAUSE I KNOW I SHOULD HAVE JUST COME HOME. I SAID THAT ALREADY.

* YELLING *

JESUS, WEBER, I KNOW! THE ONLY PLACE I WANT TO BE RIGHT NOW IS WITH YOU, BUT MY CAR WILL BE IN SOME IMPOUND YARD TOMORROW IF I LEAVE IT AT THE BAR!

I WOULD HAVE BEEN HERE.

* YELLING *

......

* SOB *

* GROAN *

OKAY, I'LL BE RIGHT THERE. TELL ME WHERE THE BAR IS. I'LL GO GET IT AND DRIVE TO YOU.

I THOUGHT HE WENT TO A SMALL GET-TOGETHER, BUT IT SEEMS TO BE A PARTY.

* LOUD MUSIC *

* BOISTEROUS *

* BUSTLING *

* LOUD MUSIC *

WEBER!

* RUNNING *

* HOLDING TIGHT *

콰악

* PANTING *

하아아

하악 * GASP *

IO, KEEP
GOING.

LET'S GO HOME.

WEB, JUST TAKE
ME INTO THE
BATHROOM, OKAY?

Chapter 19

YOU'RE REALLY DRUNK.

I WAS WORRIED THAT MAYBE YOU MIGHT'VE STARTED KISSIN' FROGS AGAIN.

CHRIST, WEBER, YOU'RE MY PRINCE, IDIOT. YOU WERE NEVER A FROG.

YOU SURE ABOUT THAT?

I'M YOUR PRINCE?

YES. IT'S ALWAYS BEEN YOU. BUT PLEASE, LET'S JUST GO HOME NOW.

WHY?

BECAUSE I NEED YOU, AND YOU WON'T FUCK ME HERE.

NO, I WON'T, BUT I WILL PUT YOU OVER THE COUCH IN THE LIVING ROOM WHEN WE GET HOME IF YOU CAN'T MAKE IT TO THE BEDROOM.

* SQUEEZING *

WEBER!

* YELLING *

* SOB *

I CAN'T...
I DON'T WANT
YOU TO GO.

WHAT'S WRONG,
TALK TO ME.

I WANT YOU
TO STAY. GOD,
WEBER, I HAVE
NEVER NEEDED
ANYONE LIKE
I NEED YOU.

* CRYING *

* TEARS
DRIPPING *

I NEED YOU TOO.

I LOVE YOU.

YOU DO?

OF COURSE I DO, DON'T BE STUPID.

* HUGGING TIGHT *

WEBER!

* SQUEEZING HARD *

I FINALLY UNDERSTOOD THAT CYRUS TRULY LOVED ME, AND NOT BECAUSE I WAS SOME ROMANTIC IDEAL, BUT BECAUSE I WAS ME.

HE RECOGNIZED HOW MUCH I LOVED HIM AND MADE ME UNDERSTAND THAT HE DIDN'T HAVE EVERYTHING UNLESS HE HAD ME.

HE WORSHIPPED THE GROUND I WALKED ON.

* SOB *

* HOLDING TIGHT *

I THOUGHT I HAD NOTHING TO OFFER...

* BUZZING *

...BUT THIS MAN NEEDED ME AND...

* BUZZING *

...I NEEDED HIM TOO.

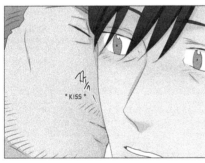

* KISS *

OH GOD, WEBER.

* PULLING BACK *

YOU HUGGED ME IN A DIFFERENT WAY.

...YOU FEEL DIFFERENT.

DO I?

WEBER, I CAN'T BELIEVE IT.

IS THAT A GOOD THING?

* LONG SIGH *

YOU'RE GOING TO STAY? YOU'RE GOING TO STAY AND LIVE WITH ME UNTIL I DIE?

I'LL PASS BEFORE YOU, IDIOT. I'M THE OLDER ONE.

WEBER!

* LAUGHING *

* JUMPING *

* PANTING *

* MOAN *

* GASP *

* GROAN *

* BUZZING *

* WHISTLING *

THAT'S ENOUGH, CYRUS. WE GOT IT.

* APPLAUSE *

HE'S YOUR MAN AND WE MUST KEEP OUR HANDS OFF HIM.

LAUGHING *

HEY.

GOD, THAT WAS HOT. I HAD NO IDEA YOU HAD THAT IN YOU, DR. BENNING.

* WHOOSH *

YOU'RE GOING TO STAY AND BE MINE.

LET'S GO HOME.

* NODDING *

YESSIR.

YOU KNOW WHAT I WANT?

TELL ME.

WHEN WE GET HOME, I WANT YOU TO HOLD ME SO TIGHT THAT I CAN FEEL YOUR HEART BEATING.

I WILL.

* STAGGERING *

* HOLDING TIGHT *

WEBER.

* BUZZING *

WILLIAM, RIGHT?

YES.

IT'S GOOD TO SEE YOU. ARE YOU STAYING THIS TIME? FROM THE LOOK ON CYRUS'S FACE, IT SEEMS LIKE YOU ARE.

YES, I DECIDED TO STAY.

I'M SO GLAD, WEB. FOR BOTH OF YOU.

WEBER?

* MOVEMENT *

OH.

I WANT US TO BE FRIENDS.

I'M THRILLED THAT YOU'RE GOING TO STAY. COME SAY A QUICK HELLO TO THE GUYS?

NEXT TIME.

* MOVEMENT *

HE'S TRASHED.

* WHISPERING *

WELL, SEE YOU SOON.

* STAGGERING *

GOD, CYRUS, YOU'RE DRUNK.

YEAH, I'M DRUNK. SO WHAT?

* SQUEEZING *

CYRUS!

I SAW THAT OVER-THE-TOP DISPLAY INSIDE. I DON'T GET AN INTRODUCTION TO THE MAN YOU PINED FOR?

JUST LET IT GO, SETH. WE'RE JUST LEAVING.

SETH... CYRUS'S EX.

SO LET ME UNDERSTAND. I WASN'T GOOD ENOUGH, BUT A HOMELESS DRIFTER IS!

HOW DOES THAT MAKE ANY SENSE?

* WHOOSH *

* SWISH *

MOVE, PLEASE.

SO, YOU'RE THE FAMOUS WEBER, HUH? I CAN'T SAY I'M IMPRESSED. STILL RIDING BULLS, COWBOY?

* SNEER *

NOPE. I ONLY RIDE CYRUS'S COCK NOW.

WEBER...!

ARE WE CLEAR?

* SPEECHLESS *

* STAMMERING *

GET THE FUCK OUT OF OUR WAY BEFORE I KICK YOUR ASS!

* STAGGERING *

* SWINGING HIS ARM *

* SURPRISED *

* FLEEING *

* FUMING *

Chapter 20

CAREFUL.

* GRUMBLING *

* STAGGERING *

HE'S REALLY DRUNK.

UGH.

HUH?

* STARTLED *

* LIFTING *

* HEAVY FOOTSTEPS *

THAT WAS THE GUY YOU SLEPT WITH WHEN I LEFT LAST TIME, HUH?

PUT ME DOWN.

WEBER! PUT ME DOWN!

HOW THE HELL DID HE KNOW I WAS A BULL RIDER?

BECAUSE I TOLD HIM ALL ABOUT YOU!

WHY WOULD YOU CARE IF I TOLD HIM?

BECAUSE IT'S PRIVATE!

* HEAVY FOOTSTEPS *

WHAT WE DO IN OUR BEDROOM IS OUR BUSINESS, AND IT WAS BEAUTIFUL AND AMAZING AND NOTHING I WOULD HAVE EVER SHARED WITH---

* STRUGGLING *

CYRUS, CALM DOWN.

* STAGGERING *

* BACK ON THE GROUND *

* FALTERING *

ARE YOU OKAY?

...I'M FINE.

I DON'T WANT HIM TO THINK ABOUT YOU LIKE THAT, LIKE HE COULD FUCK YOU, BECAUSE ONLY I FUCK YOU!

I'M SO PISSED AT YOU RIGHT NOW!

DON'T BE.

I LIKE THAT YOU'RE POSSESSIVE OF ME. IT MEANS A LOT.

YOU'RE SUPPOSED TO CLOSE YOUR EYES WHEN I KISS YOU.

BUT I'M A LITTLE BIT AFRAID I'M DREAMING RIGHT NOW.

GOD, YOU'RE SO DRUNK AND CUTE.

I AM NOT!

SO I KIND OF DON'T WANT TO STOP LOOKING AT YOU.

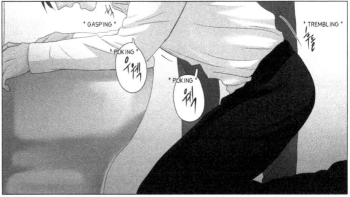

* GASPING *

* DRIPPING *

THIS IS SUPPOSED TO BE THE MOST BEAUTIFUL NIGHT OF MY LIFE.

BUT THIS WAY IT'S MEMORABLE.

DON'T CARE.

* RETCHING *

I'M DISGUSTING.

YOU'RE JUST DRUNK. DID YOU EVEN EAT ANYTHING TODAY?

* GASPING *

* WHOOSH *

HOW CAN YOU EVEN BE IN HERE?

BECAUSE ALL THIS DON'T BOTHER ME NONE.

NOW GET UP, WASH YOUR FACE, BRUSH YOUR TEETH, AND I'LL GET YOU SOME TYLENOL AND WATER.

THIS IS GROSS, BUT I'M KIND OF HUNGRY.

OKAY.

AND I WANT A SHOWER.

GOOD.

YOU TAKE A SHOWER. I'LL MAKE YOU A SANDWICH AND SOME SOUP.

THANKS.

WOW! IT LOOKS DELICIOUS.

WEBER, WHAT DO YOU PLAN ON DOING NOW THAT YOU'RE GOING TO STAY?

FOR NOW, I'M GONNA TAKE CARE OF YOUR NEPHEWS. I DON'T THINK CAROLYN'S HUSBAND IS COMIN' BACK, BUT EVEN IF HE DOES, SHE'LL STILL NEED ME.

I AGREE. ARE YOU OKAY WITH DOING THAT?

I AM. ARE YOU?

WHAT DO YOU MEAN?

WELL, YOU'RE THE ONE WHO'S GONNA HAVE TO SAY THAT YOUR LOVER IS A NANNY.

* CHOKING *

끄ㄹ윽!

* GOUGHING *

* COUGH *

FUCK!

DON'T BARF ANYMORE.

JESUS CHRIST.

WEBER, I DON'T GIVE A SHIT WHAT YOU DO.

I JUST LOVE THINKING OF YOU IN OUR HOME, JUST PUTTERING AROUND DOING NOTHING, JUST BEING WITH ME EVERY SINGLE DAY. ALL I WANT IS---

YOU WANT A FOUNDATION, RIGHT?

WHAT?

YOU WANNA BUILD. YOU WANT US TO MAKE A LIFE TOGETHER.

YES. EXACTLY.

THE OTHER DAY, WHEN I WENT WITH MICAH TO THE PSYCHOLOGIST, THE DOCTOR ASKED HIM TO DRAW SOMETHIN' THAT REMINDED HIM OF ME, AND HE DREW ME AS A MOUNTAIN.

HE DID?

HE DID, AND IT GOT ME THINKIN'...

I REALLY AM A MOUNTAIN.

Chapter 21

* NOISY *

* BUZZING *

JUST GIVE US A MINUTE.

PHILLIP, DO YOU HAVE TO GO TO THE BATHROOM?

I DUNNO, MAYBE.

WE COULD GO JUST IN CASE?

HEY, TRISTAN. WEBER, HOW ARE YOU DOING?

HEY, COACH JIM.

HOW'S YOUR DAUGHTER?

SHE'S GOOD. JUST LOST THE ONE TOOTH. THANK GOD IT WAS A BABY ONE.

THAT OTHER KID SHOULD BE OUT FOR THE YEAR. HE'S A MENACE.

OH, I AGREE. ONE RED CARD ISN'T ENOUGH OF A DETERRENT FOR HIM OR HIS FATHER.

OH, HERE HE COMES.

I'M LATE BECAUSE I MET MICAH'S TEACHER ON MY WAY HERE.

AH.

SORRY IT TOOK SO MUCH TIME.

IT'S FINE.

MANY THINGS CHANGED AFTER I DECIDED TO STAY WITH CYRUS.

YOU WANT US TO LIVE WITH CAROLYN AND THE KIDS?

* MOVEMENT *

THERE ARE SO MANY EMPTY ROOMS IN THIS HOUSE, AND HAVING CAROLYN AND THE BOYS LIVE WITH US WILL MAKE EVERYTHING EASIER.

NOW, I'M HERE, AND I AIN'T GOIN' NOWHERE. YOU CAN'T GET RID OF ME NO MATTER WHAT.

CYRUS.

HE ENDED UP AGREEING BECAUSE, ABOVE ALL, THE MAN WAS LOGICAL. IT JUST MADE GOOD SENSE.

* NOD *

* SIGH *

ALL RIGHT, I'M ON BOARD.

I'M NOT WORRIED ABOUT THAT. YOU'RE NEVER LEAVING ME.

CY WAS UNSURE BECAUSE HE DIDN'T WANT ANYTHING TO WRECK OUR RELATIONSHIP.

* KISS *

BUT I WOULD NEVER DO ANYTHING TO ENDANGER OUR RELATIONSHIP. I WOULD JUST HAVE TO PROVE IT TO HIM IN THE FUTURE.

CAROLYN HAD TO MOVE A LOT OF THINGS, BUT SHE SOLD HER OLD FURNITURE WITH THE HOUSE.

CAROLYN'S EX-HUSBAND HAD SIGNED OVER EVERYTHING TO HER IN THE DIVORCE. HE JUST WANTED HIS FREEDOM AND NOT TO HAVE TO PAY ALIMONY OR CHILD SUPPORT.

* SLEEPING *

THANK YOU, CYRUS.

IF IT WASN'T FOR YOU AND WEB, I WOULD HAVE HAD TO FIGHT HIM FOR CHILD SUPPORT, AND I DIDN'T WANT ANYTHING FROM HIM EVER AGAIN. I JUST WANT HIM TO STAY IN VEGAS AND NEVER COME BACK.

I KNOW, SWEETIE.

* WHOOSH *

WEBER!

I WOULD HAVE HAD TO GO TO COURT IF IT WEREN'T FOR YOU AND MY BROTHER.

THANK YOU FOR LETTING ME HAVE MY LIFE AND MY SELF-RESPECT. EVERYONE NEEDS HELP SOMETIME.

* SHRUG *

I LOVE YOU BOTH SO MUCH.

SHE LOVES YOU TOO MUCH IF YOU ASK ME.

HOWZAT?

MY SISTER IS ALWAYS TOUCHING YOU, HUGGING YOU, LEANING ON YOU, AND STARING AT YOU. HAVEN'T YOU NOTICED?

* GRUMBLING *

* RUSTLING *

NO WAY.

C'MERE, DARLIN'.

NO, I'M SERIOUS.

* EARNEST *

I KNOW SHE LOVES ME, BUT I ALSO THINK THAT IF I GOT HIT BY A BUS TOMORROW, SHE WOULDN'T BE ALL THAT BROKEN UP.

* TREMBLING *

WEBER!

......

* LAUGHING *

* SHAKING *

WEBER YATES!

* SNIFFLING *

OH MY GOD.

YOU'RE JEALOUS OF YOUR OWN SISTER?

COME HERE, DOC.

* GRABBING *

* FLOPPING DOWN *

YOU KNOW YOU'RE THE ONLY ONE I SEE, IDJIT.

...NICE.

I CANCELLED MY TRIP IN FEBRUARY.

WHY? YOU SHOULD GO.

IT'S TOO MUCH TROUBLE.

BUT IT WOULD BE GOOD FOR YOU TO SPEND SOME TIME HAVING FUN WITH YOUR FRIENDS.

NO. I JUST WANT TO STAY HERE.

WITH YOU.

GRIN

CYRUS PUT MY NAME ON EVERYTHING. I DIDN'T WANT HIM TO DO THAT, BUT IT WAS LOGICAL AND NECESSARY TO HIM.

IF, HEAVEN FORBID, SOMETHING HAPPENED TO ME, I WANT YOU TAKEN CARE OF AS WELL AS THE BOYS.

HE ALSO LIKED HIS NAME AND MINE TOGETHER ON ANY OFFICIAL DOCUMENTS, LIKE A DEED TO A HOUSE, A MARRIAGE CERTIFICATE, AND THINGS LIKE THAT. ALL MY FAMILY'S BELONGINGS HAD BEEN RECEIVED FROM THE STORAGE FACILITY AND WERE NOW STORED AT A NEW PLACE CLOSE BY.

FOUR MONTHS AGO, WE MADE THINGS PERMANENT AND SWORE FOREVER TO EACH OTHER.

SINCE THEN, WE WERE MARRIED AT HALF MOON BAY AND...

...I BECAME THE GUARDIAN OF CAROLYN'S CHILDREN.

TIME FLIES, BUT CYRUS STILL LOVES ME PASSIONATELY.

NOW I HAVE A FAMILY. ONE THAT I HAD NEVER HOPED TO HAVE.

THEY ARE ALL A BLESSING, ESPECIALLY CY, WHO IS MY MOST TREASURED GIFT.

AND I KNOW THAT I MATTER A LOT TO THEM.

I FINALLY UNDERSTOOD THAT THE ANSWER TO BEING A REAL MAN WAS TO BE MYSELF.

* SQUEEZING *

OH DEAR GOD, WHAT IS THAT?

IS THAT THE EASTER PROGRAM?

* COMMOTION *

* NOISY *

Chapter 22

IT'S A XYLOPHONE.

NOISY

COMMOTION

A WHAT?

MICAH PLAYS THE XYLOPHONE AND SINGS. WHERE HAVE YOU PEOPLE BEEN?

MICAH PLAYS THE XYLOPHONE?

IT'S TOO LOUD.

THAT'S WHY WEBER MAKES HIM PRACTICE IN THE GARAGE.

THAT'S WHY HE'S BEEN IN THE GARAGE?

* NOD *

* CLANG! *

* RESONANCE *

OH MY.

JESUS.

* COMMOTION *

WHY ARE YOU LOOKING AT ME LIKE THAT?

* WHOOSH *

ARE YOU KIDDING? THIS COULD DAMAGE MY CEREBRAL CORTEX.

* SHAKING HIS HEAD *

PROBABLY NOT.

I'M SORRY, WHEN DID YOU GET YOUR MEDICAL DEGREE?

I LIVE WITH A DOCTOR. YOU PICK UP A BIT.

DIIIIING!

OH DEAR GOD...

IT'S ONLY FOR THE FIRST THREE SONGS. THEN THEY SWITCH TO MARACAS.

BEFORE NEW YEAR'S, MICAH HAD STARTED TO TALK TO CY, AND WE MADE NO EVENT OF IT.

WHEN WE MADE THE TRIP UP TO SEE HIS PARENTS ON THE FIRST DAY OF THE YEAR, THEY WERE SHOCKED TO HEAR HIM TALKING LIKE IT WAS NO BIG DEAL.

HE WAS SPEAKING IN A NORMAL WAY. HIS LIFE WAS SETTLED.

EXCUSE ME.

* TAP TAP *

I'M SORRY TO INTERRUPT. DID YOU SAY ONLY TWO SONGS LIKE THIS, OR TWO MORE AND THEN THE MARACAS?

TWO MORE AFTER THIS, THEN THE MARACAS.

AH... THANK YOU. AREN'T YOU MICAH'S NANNY?

YES, MA'AM, AND YOU'RE KELLIE'S MOM.

YES.

SHE PLAYS A MEAN UKULELE. I HEARD HER PRACTICING YESTERDAY.

OH.

THAT'S RIGHT. I FORGOT THERE'S THAT TOO. THANK YOU.

* FORCED CHEERFULNESS *

* PUTTING HIS HAND DOWN *

I LOVE YOU.

I LOVE YOU BACK.

I'M STILL GOING TO KILL YOU FOR NOT WARNING ME ABOUT THE XYLOPHONE.

HAHA.

피이!!

* DIIIING! *

* STARTLED *

THAT WAS CUTE THERE, DOC.

* DIIIING! *

* DIIIING! *

* BUZZING *

WHY DOES THE EASTER PROGRAM HAVE XYLOPHONES, MARACAS, BONGO DRUMS, AND UKULELES ANYWAY?

IT'S ABOUT EXPERIENCING AND APPRECIATING DIFFERENT CULTURES THROUGH THEIR MUSIC.

IT'S WHAT?

WORLD MUSIC. YOU NEED TO OPEN YOUR MIND.

* SIDEWAYS GLANCE *

MR. YATES!

OH, HELLO. THIS IS MICAH'S ART TEACHER.

HELLO. WHAT YOU JUST SAID IS COMPLETELY RIGHT.

WE MUST ALL EXPAND OUR MINDS AND BREATHE OUTSIDE OF OUR OWN CULTURAL BOXES.

* NOD *

* CHUCKLING *

OUR OWN WHAT?

* RUNNING *

IF MICAH WASN'T AT SCHOOL OR WITH HIS MOTHER, HE WAS WITH ME.

I WASN'T GOING TO DIE ON HIM, AND NEITHER WAS HIS MOTHER OR HIS UNCLE, BECAUSE WE WERE ALL HEALTHY. HE HAD FAITH IN ALL OF US TO STICK AROUND.

MICAH DIDN'T ASK AFTER HIS FATHER, WHICH MADE ME THINK EVEN WORSE OF THE MAN. BUT THEN AGAIN, THE MAN HADN'T BEEN INVOLVED IN HIS CHILDREN'S LIVES WHEN HE WAS STILL MARRIED.

OUR LIFE WAS PERFECT, AND WE DIDN'T NEED TO BEGRUDGE HIM. WE WERE A HAPPY FAMILY.

* MOVEMENT *

* KISS *

AREN'T YOU SUPPOSED TO BE MAKING POPCORN?

YOU'RE COMPLAINING?

* MOVEMENT *

* MOAN *

NO, SIR.

* SQUEEZING *

* GASP *

* MOAN *

I WOULD JUST NOT LIKE TO BE INTERRUPTED, IS ALL.

WE WON'T BE. THE DOOR IS LOCKED, AND CAROLYN IS TAKING CARE OF THE POPCORN AND THE MOVIE. WE CAN STAY IN HERE ALL NIGHT.

WHAT BROUGHT THIS ON?

YOU'RE LEAVING ME.

* TURNING AROUND *

YEAH, FOR THREE DAYS. THE SOCCER CAMP IS DONE SATURDAY AFTERNOON. WE'LL BE BACK SATURDAY NIGHT SO WE CAN BE HERE FOR EASTER SUNDAY.

STILL.

* RUSTLING *

I DON'T LIKE IT.

Chapter 23

WATCHING YOU AND MICAH TONIGHT AT THE CONCERT---IT WAS BEAUTIFUL, WEB.

ALL THREE OF THOSE BOYS LOVE YOU SO MUCH.

AS LONG AS THEY HAVE YOU AND THEIR MOTHER...

* MOAN *

* SLIDING HIS HAN
INSIDE CYRUS'S PANTS

* GASP *

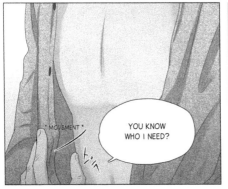

* MOVEMENT *

YOU KNOW
WHO I NEED?

* WHINE *

* RUBBING *

OH,
WEBER.

WOULD YOU
LIKE TO
GUESS?

WEBER,
I NEED
YOU.

* SQUEEZING *

* PRESSING HARD *

OH,
WEBER,
ME TOO...

* SLIDING HIS
HAND INSIDE *

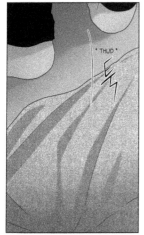

* THUD *

* PANTING *

* GROAN *

* MOVEMENT *

JESUS, JUST
WATCHING YOU
GO DOWN IN FRONT
OF ME COULD MAKE
ME COME.

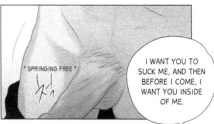
* SPRINGING FREE *

I WANT YOU TO SUCK ME, AND THEN BEFORE I COME, I WANT YOU INSIDE OF ME.

* GASP *

* GROAN

* WET *

PLEASE, WEB, DO IT LIKE YOU'LL DIE WITHOUT ME. SHOW ME THAT YOU NEED ME DESPERATELY...

* PANTING *

YOU TASTE SO GOOD.

I'M GONNA SHOW YOU EXACTLY HOW IMPORTANT YOU ARE TO ME, CYRUS.

* SLURP *

* SUCKING *

* PANTING *

* WRITHING *

WEBER.

* TUGGING *

I NEED YOU...

* PANTING *

AND IT'S KILLING ME BECAUSE I WANT YOU TO NEED ME JUST AS MUCH.

* GASP *

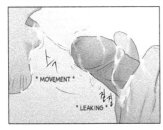

* MOVEMENT *

* LEAKING *

NOW WHO DOESN'T KNOW WHAT HE'S WORTH?

WEBER?

* SUDDENLY *

HOW COULD YOU EVER THINK YOU'RE ANYTHING BUT THE CENTER OF ALL OUR LIVES?

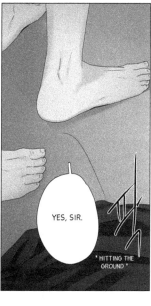

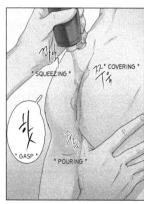

* SQUEEZING *

* COVERING *

* GASP *

* POURING *

JOLT

* PRESSING FIRMLY *

BEND OVER.

OKAY.

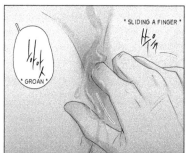

* SLIDING A FINGER *

* GROAN *

YOU MAKE EVERYTHING WORK.

* PANTING *

NEVER DOUBT IT, NEVER HAVE A MINUTE OF UNCERTAINTY. IT'S YOU, I SWEAR IT.

WEBER...

* MOAN *

* GASP *

WE ALL NEED YOU, CYRUS.

* SHIVERING *

* SWAYING *

* PANTING *

I LOVE THE OTHERS... I DO, BUT I NEED YOU, WEB, WANT YOU.

* ADDING A SECOND FINGER *

YOU WANT ME TO WANT YOU, NEED YOU?

* GASP *

WEBER!

* PANTING *

FUCK ME, PLEASE!

YOU'RE NOT READY YET.

PLEASE!

* MOAN *

* PANTING *

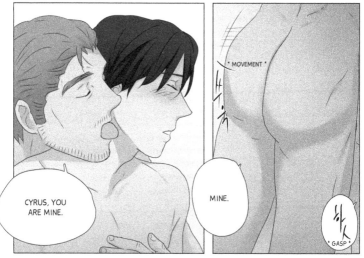

* MOVEMENT *

CYRUS, YOU ARE MINE.

MINE.

* GASP *

CYRUS WANTS ME TO PROVE THAT OUR RELATIONSHIP IS STRONGER THAN EVER AND I'M GONNA SHOW HIM.

OH, WEBER!

* RAMMING IN *

* PANTING *

CYRUS, IN THIS HOUSE, UNDER THIS ROOF, YOU SURRENDER TO ME! EVERYTHING IS MINE---YOUR FEAR, YOUR HOPES ALL OF IT.

* MOANING *

I'LL TAKE CARE OF YOU, I'LL PROTECT YOU, AND I'LL LOVE YOU NO MATTER WHAT.

* PANTING *

* RAMMING IN *

BECAUSE YOU BELONG TO ME.

YOU PROMISE?

* ROCKING *

* RAMMING IN *

I SWEAR. NOW GRAB YOUR COCK.

* SQUEEZING *

* PANTING *

SHOW ME THAT YOU MEAN IT. LET ME SEE THE RING.

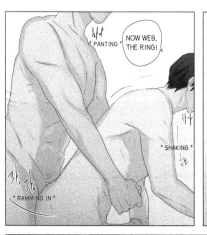

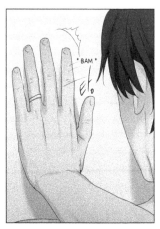

Chapter 24

* PANTING *

* PANTING *

* PANTING *

* INHALING SHARPLY *

WEBER.

YES.

* PANTING *

I DIDN'T WANT TO PUT ANY MORE ON YOUR PLATE, SO I'VE BEEN KEEPING A LOT OF THINGS TO MYSELF.

DO YOU THINK OF THIS AS OUR HOUSE?

* GASP *

YES. IT'S MORE YOURS THAN ANYONE ELSE'S.

WHEN ANY OF THE REST OF US AREN'T HERE, IT'S OKAY. BUT WHEN YOU'RE NOT HERE, IT'S EMPTY. YOU MAKE THIS HOUSE A HOME. YOU'RE THE ONE WE ALL LOVE AND NEED. YOU'RE THE STRONG ONE.

CYRUS.

* SWEEPING HIS HAIR *

IF THAT'S HOW YOU TRULY FEEL, THEN LAY ALL YOUR CRAP ON ME, ALL RIGHT? PLEASE LET ME SHOULDER IT, WHATEVER IT IS, WHENEVER IT IS. IT'S MY RIGHT AS YOUR HUSBAND, AND THE MAN YOU LOVE.

RESPECT ME ENOUGH TO TRUST ME WITH THE BULLSHIT AS WELL AS THE GOOD STUFF.

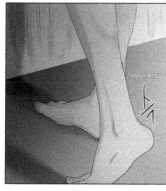

* MOVEMENT *

* FALLING WITH A THUD *

* LONG SIGH *

WAIT.

LEMME GO GET YOU SOME WATER.

" GRABBING "

LET ME ROLL AROUND IN MY ALONE TIME JUST FOR ANOTHER MINUTE.

CAROLYN AND THE BOYS WILL MOVE OUT EVENTUALLY, AND YOU'LL MISS THEM SOMETHIN' FIERCE.

I LOVE THEM ALL, AND I LOVE THEM BEING HERE. BUT I WOULD ALSO LIKE FOR YOU TO PUT ME OVER THE KITCHEN TABLE SOMETIMES TOO.

" SCREECHING "

THAT'S GROSS.

" LAUGHING "

YOU KNOW WHAT I MEAN.

WE NEED TO CARVE OUT A BIGGER CHUNK OF TIME FOR US. I'LL WORK ON IT THE MINUTE I GET BACK FROM SOCCER CAMP.

I DO.

* MOVEMENT *

I SOUND LIKE A NEEDY PIECE OF CRAP.

YOU HAVE ME AND YOU WANT ALONE TIME WITH ME. HOW IS THAT NEEDY?

BUT I HAVE TO UNDERSTAND THAT I SHARE YOU WITH FOUR OTHER PEOPLE.

* STROKING *

AND I HAVE TO KNOW EVERYTHING THAT'S GOIN' ON IN THAT HEAD OF YOURS, SO YOU HAVE TO KEEP TALKING TO ME. BECAUSE YOU THINKIN' THAT YOU'RE ANYTHING LESS THAN NECESSARY IS TOTAL CRAP.

JESUS, WEB.

* SQUEEZING *

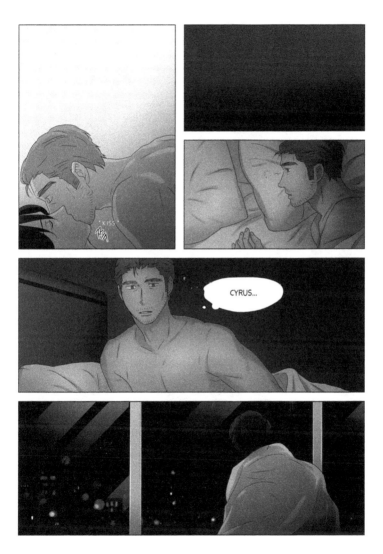

NOT BORED OF YOUR LIFE, ARE YOU? WISH YOU WERE BACK OUT THERE ON THE PROWL?

NO, I'M JUST GLAD WE GOT THINGS STRAIGHT TONIGHT.

I WANTED TO KNOW WHERE I STOOD. I'VE BEEN WONDERING FOR A WHILE, AND YOU TOLD ME.

I KNOW YOU LOVE ME AND YOU NEED ME AND THAT NOT WANTING TO BE IN CONTROL ALL THE TIME, OF EVERYTHING, DOESN'T MAKE ME WEAK.

NO, IT DOESN'T.

* NOD *

I CAN DEAL WITH YOU BEING GONE NOW THAT I KNOW WHERE I STAND.

GOOD.

YOU ALWAYS KNEW, INSIDE, DIDN'T YA?

YOU WERE THE ONLY PIECE I WAS MISSING TO MAKE MY LIFE HOW I ALWAYS WANTED.

I HOPED. I NEVER WANTED ANYTHING LIKE I WANTED YOU, WEB.

CHRIST, AIM HIGHER NEXT TIME.

정레

* SHAKING HIS HEAD *

I'M TRYING TO HAVE A MOMENT HERE!

OH, SORRY, BY ALL MEANS, HAVE YOUR MOMENT.

CYRUS.

COME HERE. I LOVE YOU.

WELL, NOW I CAN'T, DICKHEAD! YOU RUINED IT!

MARY CALMES believes in romance, happily ever afters, and the faith it takes for her characters to get there. She bleeds coffee, thinks chocolate should be its own food group, and currently lives in Kentucky with a five-pound furry ninja that protects her from baby birds, spiders, and the neighbor's dogs.

To stay up to date on her ponderings and pandemonium (as well as the adventures of the ninja), follow her on Twitter @MaryCalmes, connect with her on Facebook, and subscribe to her Mary's Mob newsletter.

Books By Mary Calmes

 ## Graphic Novels

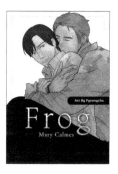

Weber Yates's dreams of rodeo stardom are about to be reduced to a ranch hand's job in Texas, unless neurosurgeon Cyrus Benning can prove that it's not Weber's job that makes him Cyrus's perfect man—it's Weber himself.

 ## Written Novels

Weber Yates's dreams of stardom are about to be reduced to a ranch hand's job in Texas, and his one relationship is with a guy so far out of his league he might as well be on the moon. Or at least in San Francisco, where Weber stops to see him one last time before settling down to the humble, lonely life he figures a frog like him has coming.

Cyrus Benning is a successful neurosurgeon, so details are never lost on him. He spotted the prince in a broken-down bull rider's clothing from day one. But watching Weber walk out on him keeps getting harder, and he's not sure how much more his heart can take. Now Cyrus has one last chance to prove to Weber that it's not

Weber's job that makes him Cyrus's perfect man, it's Weber himself. With the help of his sister's newly broken family, he's ready to show Weber that the home the the the man's been searching for has always been right there, with him. Cyrus might have laid down an ultimatum once, but now it's turned into a vow—he's never going to let Weber out of his life again.

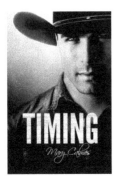

Stefan Joss just can't win. Not only does he have to go to Texas in the middle of summer to be the man of honor in his best friend Charlotte's wedding, but he's expected to negotiate a million-dollar business deal at the same time. Worst of all, he's thrown for a loop when he arrives to see the one man Charlotte promised wouldn't be there: her brother, Rand Holloway.

Stefan and Rand have been mortal enemies since the day they met, so Stefan is shocked when a temporary cease-fire sees the usual hostility replaced by instant chemistry. Though leery of the unexpected feelings, Stefan is swayed by a sincere revelation from Rand, and he decides to give Rand a chance.

But their budding romance is threatened when Stefan's business deal goes wrong: the owner of the last ranch he needs to secure for the company is murdered. Stefan's in for the surprise of his life as he finds himself in danger as well.

Sometimes the best day of your life is the one you never saw coming.

Joe Cohen has devoted the past two years of his life to one thing: the care and feeding of Kade Bosa. His partner in their PI business, roommate, and best friend, Kade is everything to Joe, even if their relationship falls short of what Joe desires most. But he won't push. Kade has suffered a rough road, and Joe's pretty sure he's the only thing holding Kade together.

Estranged from his own family, Joe knows the value of desperately holding on to someone dear, but he never expected his present and past to collide just as Kade's is doing the same. Now they've stumbled across evidence that could change their lives: the impact of Kade's tragic past, their job partnership, and any future Joe might allow himself to wish for....

Deputy US Marshal Miro Jones has a reputation for being calm and collected under fire. These traits serve him well with his hotshot partner, Ian Doyle, the kind of guy who can start a fight in an empty room. In the past three years of their life-and-death job, they've gone from strangers to professional coworkers to devoted teammates and best friends. Miro's cultivated blind faith in the man who has his back... faith and something more.

As a marshal and a soldier, Ian's expected to lead. But the power and control that brings Ian success and fulfillment in the field isn't working anywhere else. Ian's always resisted all kinds of tied down, but having no home—and no one to come home to—is slowly eating him up inside. Over time, Ian has grudgingly accepted that going anywhere without his partner simply doesn't work. Now Miro just has to convince him that getting tangled up in heartstrings isn't being tied down at all.

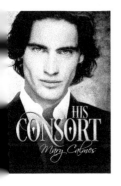

A new life in New Orleans is all Jason Thorpe had hoped: his quaint little store attracts a devoted staff and his warm, loving heart grants him a loyal circle of friends. He's perfectly content, having left behind the chill of a confusing and danger-filled night in Washington, until he discovers something unbelievable lurking in the steamy darkness of the shadowy streets of the Vieux Carré, something that turns out to be terrifying... and utterly mesmerizing.

The prince of the vampyrs, Varic Maedoc, is visiting New Orleans when he finds out the man who once helped his counselor is there in the Quarter. He thinks to simply meet and thank Jason—until he lays eyes on him. Varic's devoted himself to protect the honor of his race, and he's never wanted a mate before... but he immediately knows he must have this man, and no one else will do.

Varic may want to bring Jason safely into his world, but someone who doesn't like the human's soothing influence on vampyrs has deadly plans that would disrupt Varic's dreams. Now, unable to tell friend from foe, Jason finds himself wondering how to hold on to the prince's heart when he's fighting for his life.

FOR

MORE

OF THE
BEST
GAY
ROMANCE

DREAMSPINNER
PRESS
dreamspinnerpress.com

CPSIA information can be obtained
at www.ICGtesting.com
Printed in the USA
FFHW022251180119
50077505-54910FF